Killer Blonde

Also by Laura Levine
in Large Print:

This Pen for Hire

This Large Print Book carries the
Seal of Approval of N.A.V.H.

A Jaine Austen Mystery

Killer Blonde

Laura Levine

Thorndike Press • Waterville, Maine

Published in 2004 by arrangement with Kensington Books, an imprint of Kensington Publishing Corp.

Thorndike Press® Large Print Mystery.

The tree indicium is a trademark of Thorndike Press.

The text of this Large Print edition is unabridged. Other aspects of the book may vary from the original edition.

Set in 16 pt. Plantin by Minnie B. Raven.

Printed in the United States on permanent paper.

Library of Congress Cataloging-in-Publication Data

Levine, Laura, 1943–
    Killer blonde / Laura Levine.
      p. cm. — (A Jaine Austen mystery)
    ISBN 0-7862-6854-9 (lg. print : hc : alk. paper)
    1. Austen, Jaine (Fictitious character) — Fiction.
2. Women detectives — California — Los Angeles —
Fiction.   3. Socialites — Crimes against — Fiction.
4. Los Angeles (Calif.) — Fiction.   5. Ghostwriters —
Fiction.   6. Large type books.   I. Title.
PS3612.E924K55 2004
   813′.6—dc22   2004051780

For Mark

National Association for Visually Handicapped
---------------------- *serving the partially seeing*

As the Founder/CEO of NAVH, the only national health agency solely devoted to those who, although not totally blind, have an eye disease which could lead to serious visual impairment, I am pleased to recognize Thorndike Press★ as one of the leading publishers in the large print field.

Founded in 1954 in San Francisco to prepare large print textbooks for partially seeing children, NAVH became the pioneer and standard setting agency in the preparation of large type.

Today, those publishers who meet our standards carry the prestigious "Seal of Approval" indicating high quality large print. We are delighted that Thorndike Press is one of the publishers whose titles meet these standards. We are also pleased to recognize the significant contribution Thorndike Press is making in this important and growing field.

Lorraine H. Marchi, L.H.D.
Founder/CEO
NAVH

★ Thorndike Press encompasses the following imprints: Thorndike, Wheeler, Walker and Large Print Press.

Acknowledgments

Many thanks to my editor, John Scognamiglio, for believing in Jaine Austen — and for thinking up such a nifty title. To my agent, Evan Marshall, for being such a good listener and advice-giver extraordinaire. Thanks also to Joanne Fluke, author of the deliciously clever Hannah Swensen mysteries, for her much-appreciated generosity. And to Carlos Marrero for his terrific cover art. A special thanks to my family and friends, for their love and support. And, finally, because I know he'll be impossible to live with if I don't mention him, thanks to the cat in my life, Mr. Guy.

Prologue

My name is Jaine, and I'm a bathaholic.

Yes, it's true. I like nothing better than to tear off my clothes in the middle of the afternoon and leap into a hot bubble bath. So it's lucky I'm a freelance writer. While other working stiffs are trapped in offices, chained to their computers, I can hop into the tub any time I please.

Which is what I was doing the day SueEllen Kingsley first called me. I'd just finished writing a slogan for a new client, Tip Top Dry Cleaners (*We'll clean for you. We'll press for you. We'll even dye for you.*), and I was relaxing in a marvelous haze of strawberry-scented bubbles. The mirrors were fogged over. The radio, if I remember correctly, was playing a soulful Diana Krall love song. And my cat Prozac was perched on top of the toilet tank, licking her privates, visions of fish guts dancing in her head.

It was one of those blissful moments I often experience after I've finished a writing assignment, basking in the glow of a job well done (or done, anyway), until it dawns on me that now that the assignment is over, I'm out of work again.

I was still in the bask-in-the-glow stage when the phone rang. I let the machine get it.

"Ms. Austen." A syrupy, southern-accented voice drifted out from the machine. "SueEllen Kingsley here. I saw your ad in the Yellow Pages —"

Yippee! A prospective client!

"And I'm calling because I need a ghostwriter to help me write a book."

At the sound of the word "ghostwriter," my enthusiasm came to a screeching halt. In my experience, people who are looking for ghostwriters often fall into the "mentally unstable" category. These are people who want to tell the world about how they were abducted to the planet Clorox and forced to have sex with spatulas. Or people who believe that they're the love child of Wayne Newton and Golda Meir.

SueEllen Kingsley left her number on my machine. For a minute I considered not returning the call. But then I remembered a few pesky facts of life, like my rent and my Visa bill and my impossible-to-kick Ben & Jerry's Chunky Monkey habit.

10

Reluctantly, I hauled myself out of the tub and into a worn chenille bathrobe. Then I shuffled over to the phone and dialed.

If I'd known what I was getting into, I would've stayed up to my eyeballs in soapsuds.

Chapter
One

SueEllen Kingsley answered the phone, her voice as gooey as melted Velveeta. "Ms. Austen," she oozed, "can you hustle your fanny over to my house in an hour?"

I assured her I was an expert at fanny-hustling, and she gave me the directions to her house. Which turned out to be more like a castle. A vintage Spanish estate nestled in one of Beverly's niftiest Hills, the house was a showstopper. Its arches and balustrades and red tile roof glistened in the midafternoon sun. The whole thing was so Spanish manor-ish, I almost expected to see Zorro leap onto one of the many balconies with a rose in his teeth. But there was no sign of Zorro. The only Hispanic in sight was a gardener pruning the bougainvillea.

I drove up a circular driveway and parked my humble Corolla next to a gleaming Bentley. Then I checked my teeth in my rear view mirror for any stray pieces of lettuce left over from the Jumbo

Jack I'd picked up on my way over. Satisfied that all was clear on the dental front, I gave myself a quick blast of Binaca and tugged a few unruly curls back into my ponytail.

Finally, plucking a stray french fry from my lap, I got out of the Corolla and looked around. What a palace. The kind of place God would build if He had money.

I was beginning to regret my decision to wear my usual work outfit of jeans and a blazer. A place like this called for something a lot fancier. Like the British crown jewels and a blazer.

Why the heck was a woman with SueEllen's money calling a writer from the Yellow Pages? I'd checked her out on Google before I left my apartment, and found her name scattered on the society pages of the *Los Angeles Times*. SueEllen was apparently a partygiver and fund raiser par excellence. Surely she had access to scads of well-known writers. So why, I asked myself again, had she called anonymous old me? Oh, well. Who cared why she called? Just as long as her check didn't bounce. And from the looks of the place, I was sure it wouldn't.

I headed up the front path, and rang the bell.

Now I don't know if they have a doorbell at Versailles, but if they do, I'll bet it sounds just like the Kingsleys'. A series of mellifluous bongs resonated from inside the house. Seconds later the door was opened by a timid Hispanic maid holding a bottle of Windex.

"Hi," I smiled. "I'm Jaine Austen. I have an appointment with Mrs. Kingsley."

"Si," she said, eyes lowered, clutching her Windex to her chest. She spoke softly, in a heavily accented voice. "Mrs. Kinglsey's having her massage. She wants you to wait in the living room."

I followed her as we hiked across the foyer. A wide curving staircase with gleaming mahogany banisters ascended to the floor above. I almost expected to see Scarlett O'Hara come skipping down the steps, twirling her parasol.

The living room was huge, with hardwood floors, an exposed wood beam ceiling, and a fireplace as big as my kitchen. I took a seat in one of the many overstuffed armchairs dotted throughout the room. The maid asked me if I wanted anything to drink, and seemed relieved when I said no.

As she skittered away, presumably to do battle with dirty windows, I glanced down

14

and saw a grease stain on my blouse. Probably from the french fry that dropped in my lap. Oh, great. Now I'd have to spend the entire interview with my blazer buttoned. Which wasn't going to be easy, since I'd bought the blazer two sizes too small. It was on sale at Ann Taylor, the only one they had left, reduced seventy percent. I went ahead and bought it, figuring I'd never have to button the damn thing.

Now I sucked in my gut, and was struggling with the buttons when I heard:

"You'll never last a week."

I looked across the room and for the first time I noticed a young girl nestled in an armchair underneath a huge bay window.

She was a chubby kid, about 15, with soft brown eyes and an old fashioned Dutch Boy haircut. Something about her looked vaguely familiar. And then I realized — Good heavens, she was me — at fifteen. Not that I have brown eyes; mine are green. And when I was 15, I wasn't quite as chunky as this girl. But there was something about her that reminded me of the young Jaine Austen. Maybe it was the book she was reading. *Stiff Upper Lip* by the British humorist P. G. Wodehouse. When I was a teenager, I was crazy about his books. In fact, I still am. But it's not every day you see a teenager reading Wodehouse.

"Nobody ever lasts a week," she said, looking up at me from under her thick bangs. "Sooner or later, they all quit."

So that's why SueEllen was willing to hire a writer from the Yellow Pages. No reputable writer would work for her.

"She's nice at first, but then she turns mean. You'll see."

"So your mom's tough to work for, huh?"

The kid looked at me as if I'd just offered her a worm for lunch.

"SueEllen isn't my mother," she said with all the warmth of Christina Crawford talking about Joan. "She's my stepmother. My real mother's dead."

"I'm sorry."

"Yeah," she said. "Me, too."

And with that she picked up her book and began reading. Conversation terminated.

"Miss Austen?"

The Hispanic maid was at the door, still clutching her Windex. I only wished she had some stain remover for the grease spot on my blouse.

"Mrs. Kingsley will see you now," she said.

16

I got up to go. I tried to button my blazer, but it was no use. SueEllen Kingsley would have to accept me as I was, grease stain and all.

"Nice meeting you," I said to the kid in the chair.

"Whatever," was her jolly reply.

I followed the maid up a flight of stairs and down what seemed like an endless hallway. If I'd known how big this place was, I would've worn hiking shoes.

Halfway down the corridor, we ran into a bubbly blonde carrying a portable massage table. She weighed about as much as my right leg.

"Hi, Conchi," she said to the maid. Then she turned to me, beaming me an impossibly white smile. "I'm Larkspur O'Leary, SueEllen's masseuse."

Larkspur O'Leary? And I thought my mom was bad naming me Jaine Austen.

"You must be the new writer," she said.

"No, not exactly. I'm just here for an interview. I haven't got the job yet."

"Oh, you will. You look very capable. And besides, SueEllen's desperate."

She beamed me another smile, almost blinding me in the process.

"Here's my card." She handed me a

pastel pink business card, with her name printed in a flowery script. "I use a special method of massage that breaks down the fat cells and gets rid of cellulite." She let her glance linger on my thighs, which, I have to admit, are home to a happy colony of fat cells.

"Thanks. I'll keep that in mind."

"Well, see ya," she said. Then she started down the hallway, swinging her massage table as if it were a bag of Fritos. For a tiny thing, she was awfully strong.

"Oh, and good luck," she called back. And then she added, with a wink, "You're going to need it."

I smiled weakly and followed Conchi down the endless hallway. At last we reached our destination. Conchi opened the door to a bathroom straight out of *Architectural Digest*, gleaming with marble, gold fixtures and light streaming in from overhead skylights. At first I thought she'd taken leave of her senses. Why on earth would she be bringing me to the bathroom? Clearly the woman had been sniffing too many Windex fumes.

"Ms. Austen, I presume?"

I looked over and saw my prospective employer, SueEllen Kingsley, stretched out in a tub so big, it could hold the entire cast of *Friends*, and still have room left over for Drew Carey.

The first thing I noticed about SueEllen were her boobs. Two perfect pink globes, bobbing in the water like cantaloupes. Later I would notice her tawny hair, her tiny waist, and her fine-boned face with an unlikely smattering of freckles on her nose. But not at first. No, all I saw at first were those incredible boobs.

"Like 'em?" Sue Ellen asked, following my gaze. "They're a birthday gift from my husband."

Talk about a gift for the gal who has everything.

"Hal's a plastic surgeon. All the stars go to him. He gives great liposuction," she added, taking a none too discreet glance at my thighs.

I was getting a bit miffed at the way everybody seemed to be taking potshots at my thighs. Okay, so I'm no supermodel, but that doesn't mean I don't have feelings.

"That'll be all, Conchi," SueEllen said, waving the maid away with her loofa sponge.

Conchi scurried out of the room, like an infantryman trying to stay out of the line of fire.

"Have a seat," SueEllen said, gesturing to the toilet bowl. I sat down on the toilet lid, crossing my arms over my chest to hide the grease spot on my blouse, and trying not to look as uncomfortable as I felt.

"I hope you don't mind my interviewing you in the bathroom," SueEllen said.

"Not at all," I lied.

"But this is where I work," she said, washing between her toes. "I get my best ideas in the bathtub."

"Me, too, actually. It's where I thought up the slogan for one of my biggest clients, Toiletmasters Plumbers."

Okay, so Toiletmasters wasn't exactly a Fortune 500 company. But at the moment, it was the shining star on my resume.

"*In a rush to flush? Call Toiletmasters!* You thought of that?"

I nodded modestly; the woman was actually impressed.

"That's wonderful, honey. I can see you're just oozing with talent. Have you ever ghostwritten a book?"

"Yes," I said. "Once."

"What was it about?"

"Uh, it was sort of a . . . memoir."

Please don't let her ask me what it was called.

"What was it called?"

20

I took a deep breath, and spat it out. (Sensitive readers may want to skip the following sentence.)

"*I Was Henry Kissinger's Sex Slave.*"

"Really?" SueEllen said. "So was I!"

"What?"

"Only kidding," she said, laughing at her own gag, her incredible breasts bouncing like buoys in the ocean.

"Ha ha," I managed weakly.

"I suppose you want to know what my book is about."

"Of course."

"It's about entertaining."

I smiled a genuine smile of relief, grateful that there were no space aliens involved.

"Sounds great."

"Oh, it will be," she said, sudsing a long lean cellulite-free thigh. "I don't know if you've ever seen my name in the papers, but I'm just about the most popular hostess on the Beverly Hills party circuit. People kill for invitations to my parties. So now I'm going to share my entertaining secrets with the public. I'll give recipes and talk about how to hire a caterer and tell all sorts of marvelous anecdotes from my past. I've led a very colorful life, you know."

I didn't doubt that for a minute.

"So how about it," she said. "You interested?"

"What exactly did you have in mind as a salary?"

"Three thousand."

"I don't know," I said. "Three thousand dollars isn't much. After all, the book will take months to write."

"Not three thousand for the whole book, silly. Three thousand a week."

Suddenly, the toilet didn't seem so uncomfortable after all.

Chapter
Two

"Three thousand dollars a week?"

My best friend, Kandi Tobolowski, sat across from me at our favorite Mexican restaurant, Pacos Tacos, where everything is defiantly fried in lard, and the combination plates have been known to send healthy men hurtling into cardiac arrest.

Kandi and I have been best friends ever since we met at a UCLA screenwriting course. We hit it off right away, in spite of the fact that she's reed thin and has fabulous chestnut hair that never frizzes in the rain.

I'd told her all about my new job with SueEllen Kingsley, and now we were celebrating.

"Three thousand a week?" she said. "That's fantastic."

"I know," I said, flagging down a passing waiter.

"Garcon," I called out. "Give me a bottle of your very best champagne."

The guy looked at me like I was nuts.

23

"We don't have champagne, señorita."

"Then bring us a pitcher of your very best margaritas."

He nodded and headed off to the bar.

"Can you believe it?" I said, scooping a wad of guacamole onto a chip. "All I have to do is write down a couple of recipes, throw in a few anecdotes, and I bring home three thousand a week!"

"That's great news, sweetie," Kandi said. "But I've got even better news for you."

"What could be better than three thousand dollars a week?"

"Tommy the Termite wants to go out with you!"

"Tommy the Termite? Who on earth is that? Sounds like a mafia hitman."

"No, silly. He's an actor from my show."

Kandi is a writer for the animated cartoon series *Beanie & The Cockroach*. For those of you lucky enough to have never seen it, it's a stirring saga about a chef named Beanie and his pet cockroach, Fred.

"His name is Ted Lawson. He's very cute, and apparently he's just broken up with his girlfriend."

"Sorry, Kandi," I said. "But I'm not dating an actor/insect."

I scooped up another glob of guacamole,

while Kandi took a tiny bite off the corner of a chip. Which is why Kandi wears a size six, and I wear a size — well, never mind what size I wear. Let's just say it's somewhere in the double digits.

"What am I going to do with you, Jaine? You sit alone in your apartment night after night, and when opportunity comes knocking, you hide under the sofa cushions. Do you want to wind up a crazy old lady who gives birthday parties for her cats?"

"What, may I ask, is wrong with giving a birthday party for one's cat?"

Kandi's eyes widened. "Don't tell me you give Prozac birthday parties?"

"Yes, in fact, I do, and for your information she really enjoys them. I put a birthday candle in her can of Fancy Mackerel Guts, and afterwards we eat cake and ice cream."

Okay, so I eat the cake and ice cream. But Prozac licks the lid.

Kandi shook her head. "I can't believe you're passing up a chance to go out with a wonderful guy to stay home and work on your relationship with your cat."

"Sorry, but you're going to have to tell this termite guy I'm not interested."

"No," Kandi said. "You're going to have

to tell him. I already gave him your number."

"Kandi! How could you?"

"What's the big deal? When he calls, just say no. You've had plenty of practice."

"I will, don't worry. And besides, if he's so great, why don't you go out with him?"

"I can't." Kandi's eyes lit up with excitement. "I'm dating someone."

"Really? Who?"

"A martial arts instructor!"

"How on earth did you meet a martial arts instructor?"

"He's teaching a self-defense course at the studio. One of the producers on the lot got assaulted on the way to her car by an angry writer, and so now they're making us study self-defense. Oh, Jaine, he's such a doll. So manly and sure of himself. Unlike the cerebral wimps I usually waste my time on."

"Does Mr. Manly have a name?"

"Matt Malone. Isn't that a great name? It's so No Frills."

"How long have you been seeing him?"

"Well, he hasn't exactly asked me out yet, but I know he will."

That's Kandi for you. Ever the optimist.

"It's obvious he likes me. He keeps calling me up to the front of the class for demonstrations. Last night, I kicked him in the groin. Not really. But he showed me where to aim. God, it was sexy.

"I'm telling you, Jaine," she said, dabbing at the guacamole with the tines of her fork. "This time I've met Mr. Right."

I smiled weakly. Kandi meets an average of 2.38 Mr. Rights per month. And 2.37 of them turn out to be duds. The amazing thing, though, is that she never gives up. She sails from one guy to the next, never bloodied, never bowed. Unlike yours truly, who threw in the towel after one measly marriage.

True, it was the marriage from Hell. But lots of other women recover from bad marriages. Why didn't I? I'll tell you why: Because those other women weren't married to The Blob. That's what I call my exhusband. I didn't always call him The Blob. Back when we were still married, I called him My First Husband. I should've known I was in trouble when he wore flip flops to our wedding. I'll spare you the painful details of the rest of our four years together. Let's just say that by the time the divorce was final, I was ready to check into a convent and throw away the key.

"Here you go, señoritas."

The waiter was at our table, with a

pitcher of margaritas. He poured us each a frosty glass.

"Here's to your new job," Kandi said, "and my new relationship."

As fate would have it, neither lasted two weeks.

"Mommy's home!" I called out as I let myself into my apartment, which — for all you architecture fans out there — is a 1940s duplex in the low-rent area of Beverly Hills. Not that the rent is actually low, but it seems that way, compared to the Casa Kingsleys of the world.

Prozac raised her head from where she was napping on my best cashmere sweater and looked at me through slitted eyes.

When will you get over the ridiculous notion that you're my mother? she seemed to be saying. *In case you've forgotten, one of us is a cat, and the other a mere mortal.*

I know she doesn't like it when I call myself Mommy, but I'm the one footing the cat food bills, so Mommy it is.

"Mommy's got a new job," I said, scratching her belly. "And guess how much I'm getting paid, snookums? Three thousand lovely dollars a week! That's enough to keep you in albacore tuna morning, noon, and night."

Her eyes shot open wide. Just the mention of food can do that to her. We're a lot alike, my Prozac and I.

The phone rang, and I got it.

"Three thousand dollars a week? Congratulations!"

It was Lance Venable, my next door neighbor.

"I couldn't help overhearing," he said.

And it's true. The man has x-ray hearing. Really. Lance hears toilets flushing in West Covina. Which was pretty disconcerting when I first moved in to my apartment, but I've gotten used to it now.

"So tell me all about your new job."

And I did.

"Wow," he said when I was through. "SueEllen Kingsley. I see her picture in the society pages all the time. What amazing tits. You really saw them naked?"

"Yep. They float."

"How come nothing fun like that ever happens at my job?" he pouted. "All I get to see are bunions."

Lance is a shoe salesman at Neiman-Marcus. Tall and thin with a headful of silky blond curls, Lance has been working at Neiman's ever since I've known him.

Unlike the other shoe salesmen at Neiman's, Lance is not an aspiring actor/

director. He knows he doesn't want to spend the rest of his life selling shoes, but so far, he hasn't figured out what he does want to do. So he spends his days fondling insteps, and is kind enough to let me use his employee discount. Which means that instead of paying $500 for a pair of outrageously overpriced shoes, all I have to pay is $400. Not that I'd ever dream of paying $400 for a pair of shoes. But I could if I wanted to, thanks to Lance. And who knows? Now that I was making three thousand smackers a week, I just might.

We gabbed some more, mainly about Lance's new boyfriend, a Brentwood real estate broker.

"Jim's so great," he gushed. "I only wish you'd meet a guy, too. Straight, of course."

He babbled on about how kind/caring/handsome/loving/sexy/talented Jim was. I'd been down this road with him before, just like I'd been with Kandi, and I knew that as sure as Prozac would wolf down her next meal, there'd be heartbreak ahead. When it comes to picking boyfriends, apparently men are just as clueless as women. Which is why I for one am perfectly happy with a cat as my significant other.

Finally, Lance wound down about the Joys of Jim, and we hung up. I headed to

the kitchen to get some kitty treats for
Prozac and some Ben & Jerry's for me.
Then I checked my e-mail. Nothing except
an offer to have hot cybersex with a
woman named Brandi. And some letters
from my parents. I decided to read my parents' letters in the morning. I didn't want
anything to bring me down off my three-
thousand-dollar-a-week high.

Don't get me wrong. I love my mom and
dad. But frankly, they're — how can I put
this gently? — they're stark raving bonkers.
To look at them, you'd think they're just an
average sixtysomething couple living in a
retirement community in Tampa, Florida.
But the truth is their lives are straight out
of a soap opera. Somehow they always
seem to be in the middle of a crisis, a crisis
they expect me to solve. I've read about
people like my parents, people who don't
feel alive unless they're swirling in a mael-
strom of drama.

Daddy is the main culprit. This is a guy
who can take a perfectly ordinary day and
turn it into an episode of *Survivor*. As my
mom often says, "Daddy doesn't have ul-
cers. He's just a carrier."

Mom's only major lapse into nuttihood
(aside from marrying Daddy) is her fanatic
devotion to the Home Shopping Club. The

woman has enough cubic zirconia to light up Times Square.

But enough about my parents. I'm sure you've got parents of your own to worry about. The point is, I'd had a good day and I wanted to keep it that way. I wasn't in the mood for a domestic crisis, or one of Daddy's bad e-mail jokes. I'd definitely save their letters for tomorrow.

Instead, I settled into bed with Ben, Jerry, and Prozac. The four of us happily watched an old Doris Day movie. At the beginning of the movie, Doris is a sensible woman, happy to be alone and independent. Not moping around, dreaming of having a man in her life. Why couldn't Kandi and Lance be more like me and Doris? But then, of course, Doris falls head over heels in love with Rock Hudson and defects to the Lance/Kandi camp.

I thought about Lance and Kandi, and their quest for Mr. Right.

"What do you think?" I said, scooping Prozac up into my arms. "Are they the smart ones for trying? Am I a fool for holing myself up in the apartment with you? Should I give it one more chance and go out with that guy from Kandi's show?"

Prozac purred in my arms, doing her best to look adorable. *Of course you're better off holed up here with me. Who wouldn't be?*

The phone rang. It was Lance.

"What guy from Kandi's show?"

I told him what little I knew about Tommy the Termite.

"Promise me you'll go out with him," he said. "I won't hang up till you promise."

So I promised, and we hung up. I turned out the light, Doris and Rock still flickering in the background.

Maybe I would go out with Mr. Termite. And maybe one of these days when I talked to a man in bed, there wouldn't be a wall between us.

YOU'VE GOT MAIL!

To: Jausten
From: Shoptillyoudrop
Subject: You'll Never Guess What Your Father's Done Now

Well, honey, I hope things are fine in Los Angeles, because they sure aren't fine here in Florida. You'll never guess what your father's done now. He's gone and bought a toupee.

It wouldn't be so bad if he'd bought a regular toupee or joined the Hair Club for

Men like a normal human being. But no, your father bought the darn thing at a thrift shop. That's right. He bought a *used toupee!*

We were at the thrift shop donating some clothing, when suddenly I looked up and saw Daddy with this ratty brown monstrosity on his head. I swear, Jaine, it looks just like squirrel fur. I begged him not to buy it, but you know how stubborn your father can be once he makes up his mind.

"Where am I going to find another toupee like this?" he asked. "Try the city dump," I said. But he ignored me and bought it anyway. He insisted on wearing it out of the store. I was so darn angry I didn't even tell him that the price tag was dangling down his neck.

And now he's strutting around like he's God's gift to women. He thinks people are staring at him because he looks "dashing," when the truth is they're staring because he looks like a recent escapee from a lunatic asylum.

Today at the Tampa Vistas Clubhouse, old Mrs. Farraday took one look at the toupee and said, "What a cute hat. Just like the one Omar Sharif wore in *Dr. Zhivago.*"

You'd think your father would be embarrassed. But no. He says Mrs. Farraday is senile and wouldn't know a quality toupee if it sat in her lap. Even worse, now he thinks he looks like Omar Sharif.

Honestly, Jaine, with that toupee on, your father is a totally different person. It's like living with a stranger. A stranger with a dead squirrel on his head. I told him I absolutely refused to have "dipsy doodle" with him if he wore that damn thing to bed. And so for the time being at least, he's taking it off at night.

Love from,
Mom

To: Shoptillyoudrop
From: Jausten
Subject: Try Not to Worry

Please, Mom, the less I know about you and Daddy "dipsy doodling," the better.

Try not to worry. Daddy's always trying new things. Sooner or later, he gets tired of them. Remember the time he bought that case of "factory seconds" self-tanning lotion and he was convinced he looked like George Hamilton until his skin turned orange?

To: Jausten
From: Shoptillyoudrop

Yes, I remember. We're still paying the dermatologist's bills.

To: Jausten
From: DaddyO
Subject: Good news

Hi, Cookie!

Did Mom tell you the good news? I bought a toupee. A top quality hairpiece. And what a difference it makes. I look years younger, and not only that, it keeps my head warm, too. Especially in air conditioned restaurants. I'll bet I won't catch half as many colds as I used to.

And I don't mind admitting, I'm getting lots of interested looks from the ladies. One of the gals at the clubhouse told me I looked just like Omar Sharif.

I'm afraid your mother is jealous of all the attention I'm getting. She makes fun of me because I bought the toupee at a thrift shop, but look who's talking. This is a woman who buys steaks from the shopping channel. Every supermarket in town sells steaks, but no, your mother has to buy them from the television. And she makes fun of me because I bought my hair at a thrift shop?

Take care, honey.

Your loving,
Daddy

PS. Here's a cute joke I heard at the clubhouse:

What goes CLOP CLOP, BANG BANG, CLOP CLOP?

An Armenian drive-by shooting!

To: DaddyO
From: Jausten

Thanks for the joke, Daddy. But I think it's supposed to be an Amish drive-by shooting. Because their horses go clop clop. Get it?

About your new head of hair: Are you sure you want to be wearing a used toupee? I mean, you have no idea who might have worn it before you. What if they had a scalp disease?

To: Jausten
From: DaddyO
Subject: Previously Owned

First of all, honey. My toupee is not "used." It's "previously owned." The lady at the thrift shop told me it belonged to Burt Reynolds! Either him, or Sam Donaldson. And no need to worry about germs. I've already sprayed it with Lysol.

To: Jausten
From: Shoptillyoudrop
Subject: Self-respecting germ

Your father just sprayed his toupee with Lysol. He needn't have bothered. No self-respecting germ would be caught dead in that wig.
　I've simply got to think of a way to get rid of it.

Your desperate,
Mom

Chapter
Three

I sat on SueEllen Kingsley's toilet bowl with a sense of foreboding. Not about the book. After five minutes listening to SueEllen prattle, I knew her book (*At Home With SueEllen*) would never see the light of day. Not with recipes that began, *"Have your maid debone a turkey . . ."* This was a woman who probably needed directions to get to her kitchen.

No, I was worried about my father. Ever since my parents retired to Florida, Daddy's been acting nuttier than ever. Last year, for example, he was convinced my mother was having an affair with one of the hosts from the Home Shopping Club. And now this business about buying a toupee at a thrift shop. What sort of person buys a used toupee? I only hoped he wasn't going to wind up one of those crazy old men who take out their dentures in restaurants. Oh, well. There was no use worrying about it. With my parents living 3,000 miles away in Florida, there was nothing I could do.

I forced myself to listen to SueEllen, who was stretched out in the tub, rambling on about her childhood in the Deep South.

"We may not have had much money," she said, "but from an early age I learned the art of gracious living."

She picked up a pumice stone from a bath tray and began scraping away at her calluses. In addition to the pumice stone, her bath tray held such grooming necessities as a bottle of Cristal champagne, a Walkman TV, and a half-eaten salad. I eyed her salad covetously. Mainly because I was starving.

I'd shown up at one o'clock that afternoon, as instructed. Conchi fixed us lunch, eensy weensy turkey Cobb salads, with hardly enough turkey to feed a flea. I snarfed mine down in nanoseconds, sitting on the toilet bowl. SueEllen barely nibbled at hers. Now it was going on four o'clock and I was ready to eat the wallpaper.

"Mother and Dad came from old Southern aristocracy," SueEllen said, flicking the dead skin from her calluses into the water. "By the time I came along, the family money was pretty much gone. Mother clung to the old traditions, though, and passed them on to me. She taught me how to make chicken and dumplings and mint juleps and sweet little lavender sachets. I was a rebel, though. Back then, I was more interested in boys than good manners."

She looked up from her pumice stone and frowned.

"How come you're not writing any of this down?"

"Because Margaret Mitchell already wrote it. It's called *Gone With the Wind.*"

Okay, so I didn't really say that.

"I'm sorry," I smiled. "It was just so interesting, I guess I forgot to take notes."

I scribbled down the stuff about the lavender sachets and dumplings. Any minute now, I expected her to tell me about her Mammy, and them cotton fields back home.

"Of course," she said, "the biggest influence in my life was my Aunt Melanie."

She reached for her champagne, and took a sip. I'd long since polished off the Diet Coke Conchi had served me.

"Aunt Melanie married well and had scads of money. She threw the most marvelous parties, and I never forgot them. Yes, I guess you could say Aunt Melanie was the one who taught me everything I know about party planning."

So I wrote that down, too, wondering if

she'd notice if I reached over and filched some croutons from her salad. I wouldn't have minded another Diet Coke, either. And a cushion. I was getting a mighty sore tush from sitting on the toilet for three hours. SueEllen had a bathroom the size of a football stadium; why on earth couldn't she at least bring in a chair for me?

SueEllen droned on about Aunt Melanie, and her recipe for bourbon pecan balls. I was alternately taking notes and fantasizing about a cheeseburger with fries, when I glanced out the window and saw an elderly man standing on the balcony of the house next door. Normally I don't get upset when elderly men stand on their balconies. But this man was looking through a telescope that just happened to be pointed straight at SueEllen's boobs.

"SueEllen," I said. "I don't want to alarm you, but your neighbor is spying on you."

"Oh, that's old Mr. Zeller," she said, sipping her champagne, not the least bit perturbed. "He's a retired astronomy professor. Used to teach at Caltech. Don't worry. He's harmless."

"Yoo hoo, Mr. Zeller!" She sat up straight in the tub, giving him an unobstructed view of her boobs.

And then she blew him a kiss.

Good Lord. She was actually getting off on this.

Now *that* would make an interesting chapter for her book. She could call it *Entertaining the Neighbors.* At least we wouldn't have to bother with recipes.

An hour later, SueEllen was still strolling down memory lane. And I was ready to strangle her. I hadn't been off that damn toilet seat all afternoon, except to add hot water to her tub.

"You don't mind, do you?" she'd asked. "I'm so comfortable in the water, I hate to move."

Heavens, no. I wouldn't want her to exert herself by actually having to turn on a faucet. So I'd smiled weakly and turned on the hot water. I felt like a slave girl in one of those old 50s biblical epics.

I checked my watch. 5:10. I couldn't believe it. The woman was about to break the Guinness record for World's Longest Bath. Even I don't stay in the tub for four hours at a stretch. But here she was, still soaking, and still yapping. By now, of course, I was famished. I would've sold my soul for a Tic Tac.

Finally, after what seemed like hours but

was probably only ten minutes, SueEllen called it a day, and got out of the tub.

"Hand me my robe, will you, dear?" she said, flaunting her fabulous body. Not an ounce of fat anywhere. I wondered if she'd had any of it sucked away by her plastic surgeon husband.

Just as she was tying the belt on her robe, a buzzer sounded. SueEllen crossed to a control panel above her bath and pressed a button.

"Yes, who is it?"

A young man's voice filtered through a speaker. "It's me, SueEllen. I forgot my key."

"My stepson Brad," SueEllen whispered to me. "Always forgetting his key."

"Okay," she said, pressing a button. "Come on in."

Once again, my mind boggled. What sort of person has an intercom for their bathtub?

"Isn't this clever?" she said. "I had it installed so in case the maid isn't around, I don't have to get out of the tub to answer the door. I don't know what I'd do without it."

Yeah, we all know how irritating it is when the maid isn't around to answer the door.

"Hey, I've got an idea," she said. "Why don't you stay for dinner? You can meet my husband and stepchildren — Brad and his sister Heidi."

"Actually, I think I've already met Heidi."

SueEllen shook her head, in a gesture that was meant to portray sympathy.

"Poor Heidi. Such a troubled child. Terrible weight problem. I'm sure you can relate."

Ouch. That one hurt.

"My heart goes out to the poor darling," she said, scrutinizing her face in a magnifying mirror, and squeezing a blackhead. "So I've been helping her with her diet. One of these days, she's going to look just fine.

"So how about it?" she said. "Will you stay for dinner?"

Was she kidding? If I had to listen to one more word about Aunt Melanie and her damned pecan balls, I'd go bonkers. No way was I staying for dinner. I'd head straight home with a pitstop at McDonald's.

"We're having beef bourguignon," SueEllen said.

My salivary glands sprung into action.

"With cherry cobbler for dessert," she added.

"Sure." I gulped. "Sounds great."

SueEllen plunked me down to wait in her oak-paneled den while she got dressed for dinner. The first thing I did was call Prozac. I once read that animals are comforted by the sound of their owner's voice on the phone. Cooing into my answering machine, I told Prozac that I'd be late and that there was dry food in her bowl, and to please not pee on my pillow as she sometimes does when she's pissed at me for being late. I told her to be a good girl, then made a few obnoxious kissy noises and hung up.

I tried to look over my notes, but I couldn't concentrate. All I could think of was food. The smell of beef bourguignon simmering on the stove was driving me crazy. I ransacked my purse for something to eat, but all I came up with was an old Doublemint gum wrapper, which I'm ashamed to say I licked clean.

Then I glanced over at the wet bar and saw my salvation. A bowl of hard candies was sitting on the counter, beckoning to me. I raced over, only to discover they weren't real candies, but made of glass. What sort of sadist has glass candies out on display to fool unsuspecting guests? The same sort of sadist who makes her writers sit on the toilet bowl, that's who.

I decided to search behind the bar. Surely there'd be something to eat. Some nuts, maybe, or chips. But no. All I saw were bottles of booze. For a brief instant I considered chugalugging some Grand Marnier, but I couldn't risk showing up tipsy at the dinner table.

I opened the mini-fridge. Nothing but white wine. Good heavens, these people were annoying. With all their millions, couldn't they afford a measly bag of potato chips?

And then I found it. Way in the back of a cupboard, behind a stack of cocktail napkins: a jar of macadamia nuts. Macadamia nuts! I felt like Columbus discovering America, or Colonel Sanders discovering Extra Crispy Fried Chicken.

I grabbed the jar and tried to open it, but the Easy Open Lid wouldn't budge. Lord knows how long it had been sitting there in the cupboard. Maybe it was permanently welded shut. I wanted to bang the lid on the counter to loosen it, but I was afraid I'd make too much noise. So I ran it under hot water in the tiny wet bar sink. It took forever for the water in the tap to finally turn hot, but at last it did, and I held the jar under the steamy water. Then

I gave it another try. Still no luck. This was ridiculous. This jar was shut tighter than a bank vault. Somebody ought to write an angry letter to the Easy Open Lid people about the concept of truth in advertising.

I tugged at that jar with every ounce of strength I possessed, and at last the lid flew open. That was the good news. The bad news was that the nuts came flying out of the jar and landed all over the carpet.

I got down on my hands and knees and started gathering the nuts, cursing myself for agreeing to stay for dinner.

"Having fun?"

I looked up and saw SueEllen's step-daughter standing in the doorway, peering at me through those thick bangs of hers.

"Oh, geez. This is so embarrassing. You see, I got a little hungry, and —"

"Don't worry," she said, smiling shyly. "I'll help." Then she got down on her knees and started picking up nuts.

"Thanks so much," I said. "This is awfully nice of you."

"I bet the Calorie Cop didn't feed you all day," she said, plunking nuts into the jar.

"Just a tiny salad and a Diet Coke."

"I told you she'd be hell to work for.

You're lucky you got the salad."

We scooted around on all fours, gathering the macadamias. Finally, we rounded them all up. I looked down into the jar hungrily. I didn't care if they'd been on the carpet. I still wanted them.

"Look, I hope you won't think this is too disgusting, eating off the floor, but I've got to have some of these nuts. I'm starving."

"Help yourself," she shrugged.

I dusted some off and was just about to pop them in my mouth when I heard a voice warn me, "I wouldn't eat those if I were you."

I looked up and saw a handsome young guy, about 18. This was undoubtedly Brad, the stepson who forgot his keys.

"I had sex on that carpet last night."

I dropped the nuts back in the jar. That hungry, I wasn't.

Brad ambled into the room, leaving a trail of spicy aftershave in his wake. As he stretched himself out on the den's leather sofa, I took in his dark curly hair, cobalt blue eyes, and lean young body. The kid was a knockout and he knew it. I could easily picture him having sex on the carpet, or anywhere else for that matter.

"You must be SueEllen's new writer," he said.

"Yes. I'm Jaine Austen. Like the author. Only with an 'i' in Jaine."

He looked up at me, puzzled. "What author?"

Obviously the kid was no Class Valedictorian.

"Jane Austen," Heidi said with a sigh. "She wrote *Pride and Prejudice*."

"Like I care," he said, picking up a Ferrari brochure from the coffee table.

"My name's Heidi," Heidi said. "And this is my bad-mannered brother Brad."

"Nice to meet you," I said.

Brad didn't bother to look up from his Ferrari brochure.

"Dad's going to get me a Ferrari for a graduation present," he said.

"Fat chance," Heidi said. "SueEllen will never let him spend that kind of money on you."

His brow furrowed in annoyance.

"Who says?"

"Get real, Brad. Don't you know by now that all the big bucks in this house are spent on SueEllen?"

"You're nuts," he said. "Dad'll get it for me."

"Dream on."

At which point, we heard the sound of high heels clacking on hardwood.

50

"It's SueEllen," Heidi warned. "Better put that away."

I looked down and realized I was still holding the macadamia nuts. I scampered over to the wet bar, and shoved them into the cupboard, just seconds before SueEllen came sashaying into the room in skin tight capris and a low cut spandex T-shirt.

"Hi, kids," she said, flashing what I suspected was a rare smile at them. "Brad, sweetheart, feet off the sofa, please."

Brad grudgingly flopped his feet down from the sofa.

"Well," she said, smiling brightly, "is everybody hungry?"

Talk about your rhetorical questions.

"Shall we?" she said, gesturing to the door. Then her face puckered in annoyance.

"What's this?" She bent down and picked up a macadamia nut that had managed to escape our clutches.

SueEllen eyed Heidi coolly.

"Is this yours?" she asked, holding out the offending nut.

Heidi looked down at the carpet, saying nothing. What a nice kid, I thought. Clearly, she didn't want to get me in trouble.

"How many times have I told you?" Sue Ellen said, tapping her foot in annoyance.

"No Between-Meal Snacks!"

"Actually," I piped up. "It's mine."

"It is?" SueEllen looked almost disappointed, as if she'd been looking forward to ragging on Heidi, and I'd robbed her of the opportunity.

"Well, technically," I said, "it's yours. I found a jar of nuts in your wet bar. I'm sorry I opened it without asking, but I was awfully hungry."

"You were?" she asked, amazed that anyone could possibly be hungry after the elaborate 10-calorie lunch she'd served.

"Oh, well," she said. "No matter. Let's go satisfy that appetite of yours, shall we, Porky?"

Okay, so she didn't really call me Porky, but I knew that's what she was thinking.

And as we followed SueEllen out the door, Heidi turned to me and smiled. I smiled back, happy that there was at least one person in the Kingsley clan that I could relate to.

Hal Kingsley was an older version of Brad — tall and craggy with wavy hair graying at the temples, a Marlboro Man who'd gone to med school. He sat at the head of the huge mahogany dining table, nursing a martini, silent and distant, like a guest who didn't know the other people at the table very well.

SueEllen was at the foot of the table, barking orders to Conchi. Heidi and Brad sat across from me, looking like they'd sell their souls for an In 'N Out Burger.

Conchi scurried around with our salad plates, eyes downcast, her dark hair falling forward on her face like a curtain she was trying to hide behind. The salad was endive and watercress in a raspberry vinaigrette dressing. It was about as filling as a piece of dental floss.

The beef bourguignon on the other hand, looked spectacular. Generous chunks of meat in a lovely brown potato-and-carrot studded sauce. Conchi came out of the kitchen with two heaping platefuls, and my salivary glands sprung into action.

Unfortunately, the heaping plates went to Hal and Brad. Heidi, SueEllen and I got portions the size of rice cakes. Heidi and I snarfed ours down with lightning speed; I practically scraped the design off my plate trying to finish every last drop. Once again, SueEllen nibbled at her food. It was all I could do to keep from grabbing one of her potatoes.

Needless to say, nobody asked me if I wanted seconds.

What's worse, SueEllen actually expected me to be taking notes. That's right. SueEllen wanted it to be a "working dinner." While everybody ate, she picked up where she left off in the bathtub, in the saga of SueEllen.

"I'll just give you the broad strokes now," she said, spearing a particle of carrot. "We'll fill in the details later."

And so she was off and running, dominating the conversation with a non-stop commentary about how she left the South and moved to L.A. and became a model, and later a game show hostess, until she finally hit the jackpot and became Mrs. Hal Kingsley. When she came to the part about her job as a game show hostess, she demonstrated how she used to point out the contestants' prizes, by making a flamboyant "L" with her arms. Left arm up in the air, right arm pointing to the imaginary prize. I only hoped she didn't expect me to write about Game Show Hostess Positions in the book.

When everyone else had finished their beef and their eyes were glazed over with boredom, Hal piped up.

"SueEllen, honey, you haven't touched your dinner."

Indeed she hadn't. Her dollop-sized portion was still sitting there in the middle of her plate. Reluctantly, she shut up and started eating.

Brad took advantage of her blessed silence.

"Hey, Dad," he said. "I got the new Ferrari brochure today."

SueEllen looked up from the pea she was pushing onto her fork.

"Ferrari? What Ferrari?"

Hal grinned sheepishly. "I sort of promised Brad a Ferrari for graduation."

"A Ferrari for an eighteen year old?" she said, abandoning the pea. "That's ridiculous. He should be happy with a BMW like every other teenager in Beverly Hills."

"But Dad promised me I could get one."

"Can you imagine what the insurance will cost?"

Hal's face clouded over with doubt. "I hadn't thought of that."

"But Dad, you promised."

"I did promise him, SueEllen."

"Well, if that's your decision," SueEllen said, a veil of ice descending in the room.

Hal finished what was left of his martini in a single gulp.

"Maybe SueEllen's right, Brad. I've got to think it over."

SueEllen ate her pea with a satisfied smile.

Why did I get the feeling that Brad Kingsley was about to kiss his Ferrari goodbye?

Finally, SueEllen finished picking at her beef bourguignon, and Conchi was allowed to bring in dessert. Cherry cobbler, as advertised. Once again, Conchi served Hal and Brad hearty portions, after which she brought out golfball-sized portions for the gals. She put mine in front of me with an apologetic smile, then gave SueEllen hers.

Then, just as she was about to serve Heidi, SueEllen snapped: "No, Conchi. No cobbler for Heidi. She's too fat."

Heidi sat rigidly in her chair, flushed with humiliation. She looked to her father for help, but he kept his eyes on his cobbler.

"Then may I be excused?" she said, voice wavery with impending tears.

"No, you may not," SueEllen said, scooping up a spoonful of her cobbler. "You're going to have to learn to resist temptation, young lady."

And with that she put her spoonful of cobbler to her lips and ate it with gusto.

"Mmm, delicious," she said, licking her lips.

Good heavens, the woman really was a sadist.

"What do you think, Jaine? Isn't it delicious?"

"Actually," I said, "I'm not hungry."

And it was true. For the first time all day, I'd lost my appetite.

"Just taste it," SueEllen cooed. "It's divine."

"No, if Heidi can't have any, I don't think I want any, either."

Her smile froze. If her boobs hadn't been silicone, they would've been quivering in indignation. This is it, I thought. This is where she sends me packing.

But, no. I guess she decided she didn't want to go through the bother of finding another writer willing to sit on her toilet bowl.

"Oh, well," she said with a shrug. "*Chacun à son goût.*"

That's French for "I'll get you later, bitch."

I drove home from the Kingsleys, unable to stop replaying the scene I'd witnessed at dinner. I'd seen SueEllen in full bitch mode, and it was not a pretty picture. Poor Heidi. My heart went out to her.

I let myself in my apartment, filled with

gratitude that I wasn't a part of that dys-functional family. Okay, so maybe my father bought used toupees, and maybe my cat occasionally peed on my pillow, but we loved each other, and that was all that counted. I scooped up Prozac from where she was napping on a pile of freshly laundered towels, and hugged her to my chest, feeling her purr. I carried her to the bedroom, still holding her to my chest like a furry vibrator.

"Oh, Prozac. How nice. You didn't pee on my pillow, after all."

No, as I was to find out very shortly, she peed in my slippers instead.

Chapter
Four

The next day I was back on toilet bowl patrol. This time I knew enough to eat lunch before coming over, so I didn't mind when Conchi served us a few radiccio leaves masquerading as a salad.

I was more convinced than ever that SueEllen's book didn't stand a chance of getting published. The recipes were either too elaborate (. . . *marinate your pheasant for two days in a clay pot* . . .) or too expensive (. . . *Take three pounds of beluga caviar.* . . .) And those endless anecdotes. All that mushy goo about her Aunt Melanie and life among the magnolia blossoms. Did she really think people wanted to read about a woman whose biggest accomplishment in life was pointing out prizes on national TV?

No, the book was bound to be a bust. And frankly, my dear, I didn't give a damn. I couldn't stop thinking about how cruelly SueEllen had treated Heidi at dinner. Maybe that's why all her other writers quit.

Maybe they, too, got a glimpse of life behind the scenes *At Home With SueEllen.*

A part of me (the noble sensitive part) felt like quitting, but another part of me (the part who likes being able to pay the rent) couldn't pass up three thousand dollars a week. So I stayed put on the toilet, taking notes and counting the minutes until it was over.

At last, SueEllen set me free. I practically flew downstairs and out to my car. I wondered if I'd run into Heidi, but she was nowhere in sight.

After a cozy dinner at home (Progresso minestrone for me and Fancy Fish Entrails for Prozac), I headed off to the Shalom Retirement Home, where I teach a class in memoir writing. It's a small class, only about a half dozen students. Most of them women in their eighties. All of them with a lot to say, and not much time left to say it. Sometimes they drive me nuts, but all in all, teaching that class is one of the most gratifying things I've ever done in my life.

When I showed up at the Shalom conference room that night, a rose was waiting for me at my place at the head of the table. It was a gift from Mr. Goldman, the lone man in my class. A short man with an uncanny resemblance to Mr. Magoo, Abe

Goldman has a flaming crush on me, a fact that he doesn't bother to hide. He's always bringing me little tokens of his affection — an apple, a stick of sugarless gum, a free sample of cereal that came with his morning paper. Tonight, it was a rose.

"For you, cookie," he said with a wink. At least I thought it was a wink. Mr. Goldman has a chronic tic so I can never quite tell when he's winking or blinking.

"How nice, Mr. Goldman. Thank you."

Mrs. Pechter, a powdery woman with bosoms the size of throw pillows, shot him a look of utter disdain.

"He picked it off a funeral wreath," she said.

"Oh?" I quickly put the rose back down on the table.

"Poor Esther Sobol died," Mrs. Rubin said. "We went to the funeral today."

Mrs. Rubin was a tiny birdlike woman. Although they had their share of quarrels, she and Mrs. Pechter were best friends. I always thought of Mrs. Rubin as Laurel to Mrs. Pechter's Hardy.

"Can you believe it?" Mrs. Pechter shot a look at Mr. Goldman. "He picked a flower from a funeral wreath."

"So what?" Mr. Goldman shrugged. "You think Esther's gonna notice?"

61

"Maybe Esther won't, but God will."

"Oh, please," Mr. Goldman snorted. "With all the crazy things going on in the world, you think God cares whether or not I picked a rose from Esther Sobol's funeral wreath?"

He had a point there.

"Well, class," I said quickly, eager to avert a verbal slugfest, "who wants to read first?"

Every week, my students bring something they've written to be read aloud to the rest of the class. Most of the time it's fairly pedestrian. *My Grandson's Bar Mitzvah. My Trip to Disneyworld. My Grandson's Bar Mitzvah in Disneyworld.* Every once in a while I get a gem of a memory that makes the whole thing worthwhile. And even on the nights when all I hear about was *My Son, The Orthodontist,* I get a kick out of these people. After eighty years on the planet, they still have the energy to put their lives down on paper. Not an easy feat, at any age.

"So who wants to read?"

Mr. Goldman's hand shot up like a piston. A retired carpet salesman, Mr. Goldman was always ready to share the latest chapter of his life's adventures. Tonight's was a stirring saga called *My Dinner with Jerry Lewis*, about the time he wound up sitting next to the comic at a Beverly Hills coffee shop. (Jerry is a big tipper, in case you were wondering.)

He finished to a round of polite applause, and then Mrs. Pechter raised her hand.

"Mrs. Pechter," I nodded. "What've you got?"

She cleared her throat, and read the title of her piece:

"Once Around the Lake, Morris."

It was one of the gems. A touching story about her husband Morris, and their summer vacations in the Catskills Mountains. Every night after dinner in the hotel dining room, Mrs. Pechter would turn to her husband and ask, *"Once around the lake, Morris?"* *"My pleasure, Rose,"* Mr. Pechter would reply. And the two of them would walk around the lake. Holding hands under the stars, they'd talk. About their day. About their kids. About their lives. "I never felt closer to him than on those walks," she read. "They were the best part of my marriage." Then one night after just such a walk, they went back to their cabin where Mr. Pechter sat down in an Adirondack chair and died.

"I thought I'd never get over it," she read,

her voice wavering with emotion, *"but eventually, I did. Maybe not completely, but enough to keep going."* Two months later, her daughter gave birth to a little boy. And they named him Morris. He grew up, Mrs. Pechter confided, to be her favorite grandson. *"A wonderful boy,"* she said, *"who takes me out for dinner every week. And after dinner, I turn to him and say, 'Once around the lake, Morris?' And he says, 'My pleasure, Grandma.' Of course, there's never a lake outside the restaurant. But we walk around the block, holding hands. And wherever my Morris is, I know he's smiling."*

When she was through, I had tears in my eyes. It was just so damn touching. What a contrast to SueEllen's blather. Would I ever, I wondered, meet a Morris of my own?

As if in answer to my question, Mrs. Pechter took me aside after class and said, "You know my grandson Morris? The one I wrote about? He's an accountant. Very comfortable."

She smiled proudly.

"That's wonderful," I said.

"And single."

"Oh?"

"I thought maybe he could call you up for a date."

My smile froze. Whoa, Nelly. Yes, I know I said I wanted to meet a Morris of my own, but I didn't mean an actual guy named Morris. Call me shallow, but my dream man is not an accountant named Morris. He's an artist named Zane, or a chef named Sergio.

"Gee, that's awfully sweet of you, Mrs. Pechter, but —"

But what? What the heck was I going to say to her? I don't date accountants named Morris?

"— but I'm seeing someone."

"You have a boyfriend?" She seemed surprised, a fact which I found vaguely insulting.

"Yes, I do."

"What does he do, this boyfriend of yours?"

"Uh, he's an actor."

It was the first thing that popped into my mind. I remembered the termite impersonator Kandi wanted to fix me up with, so I used him as my phantom boyfriend.

"An actor? Have I seen him in anything?"

"Actually, he plays a termite on a cartoon show."

"Oy," was her eloquent response. "You're dating a termite?"

What was wrong with me? Why couldn't I have said I was dating a doctor?

"Hey, you forgot your flower."

Mr. Goldman was at my side, holding out the rose from Mrs. Sobol's funeral wreath.

"Oh, right," I said, taking it gingerly.

"So how about it, cookie?" he winked/blinked. "You want to come to the movies with me on Saturday?"

Saturday night was movie night at Shalom.

"They're playing *Sleeping in Seattle*."

"*Sleepless in Seattle*, Abe," Mrs. Pechter corrected. "Not sleeping."

"Sleepless, sleeping. Who cares? You wanna come with me, cookie?"

"She can't, Abe. She's already got a boyfriend."

"She does?"

Why was everybody so damned surprised?

"In that case," he said, "I want my flower back."

He took his rose and stomped off. Mr. Goldman always gets angry at me when I turn him down for dates. But sooner or later, much to my regret, he cools off and starts hitting on me again.

I bid the other ladies goodnight, and

66

headed out the door. The last thing I heard was Mrs. Rubin saying, "She's dating a termite?"

As it turns out, I *was* about to date a termite. When I let myself into my apartment that night, the phone was ringing.

"Hi," a deep male voice said, "this is Ted Lawson."

At first, I had no idea who he was.

"Ted Lawson?"

"Kandi's friend."

"Oh. Tommy the Termite."

He laughed. "Four years studying at the Actors' Studio, and I wind up playing a termite. Which wouldn't be so bad, except that I get second billing to a cockroach."

At least he had a sense of humor about himself.

"Anyhow, I was wondering if you wanted to get together for dinner Saturday night."

This was it. The moment of truth. Was I going to stay holed up with my cat for the rest of my life? Or was I going to take a chance on love?

"Sure, I'd love to," I said, taking the leap.

And it really wasn't such a big leap. Ted seemed like a perfectly nice guy. And it was only one measly dinner. After all, I figured, how bad could it be?

Stick around for a few chapters, and you'll find out.

YOU'VE GOT MAIL!

To: Jausten
From: Shoptillyoudrop
Subject: Who's Charleton MacAfee?

Last night when your father was sleeping, I gave the toupee to the cat, hoping she'd claw it to shreds. But Taffy wouldn't go near it. She took one look at it, and hid under the sofa. I think she thought it was a possum. Of course, Taffy is scared of her own shadow. Not at all like your darling kitty Zoloft.

So this morning the dead squirrel is back on your father's head, a walking eye-sore.

What with all this to-do over Daddy's dreadful hairpiece, I forgot all about your Cousin Cindy's wedding in Ohio next week. I can't believe she's getting married and you're still single. Oh, honey, wouldn't it be nice if you tied the knot one of these days, and gave Daddy and me a little grandbaby? Sometimes I think you made a mistake divorcing The Glob.

True, he hardly got off the sofa, but he had a nice smile. Oh, well. I'm sure you know best, dear.

As for the wedding, I simply don't know how I'm going to face the relatives. With that toupee on your father's head, we'll be the laughing stock of the family. I don't suppose you could possibly break away from your work and meet me there for moral support?

Love,
Mom

PS. The strangest thing about the wedding invitation. It says, "Fred and Earlene Austen, and Charleton MacAfee, request the pleasure of your company at the wedding of their daughter Cindy . . ." Do you have any idea who Charleton MacAfee is? For the life me, I can't think who it could possibly be.

To: Shoptillyoudrop
From: Jausten
Subject: Stiff competition

Sorry, Mom, I have no idea who Charleton MacAfee is. Maybe a relative of Earlene's?

And I'm afraid I can't make it to the wedding. First, I'm starting a new job. And second, I haven't been invited.

Don't worry about being the laughing stock of the family. I think you've got some stiff competition in that department. As I recall, isn't Uncle Fred the guy who sits at the dinner table with his shotgun in his lap to protect his family from alien invaders? And isn't Aunt Earlene the one who knits booties for their dog? Compared to them, Daddy will look like Cary Grant.

To: Jausten
From: Shoptillyoudrop
Subject: Cary Grant

I suppose you're right, darling, but I doubt Cary Grant ever wore a dead squirrel on his head.

To: Shoptillyoudrop
From: Jausten

Any chance of it blowing away in a stiff wind?

To: Jausten
From: Shoptillyoudrop
Subject: I knew I could count on you!

What a good idea. I'll take Daddy for a walk on the beach. It's always windy there. Thank you, darling! I knew I could count on you.

To: Shoptillyoudrop
From: Jausten

My pleasure, Mom. And by the way, my cat's name is Prozac, not Zoloft, and my ex-husband is The Blob, not The Glob — although that has a nice ring to it, too.

To: Jausten
From: DaddyO
Subject: Positive Feedback

Hi, Pumpkin!
Hope everything is fine in sunny L.A.
   I'm happy to report that I'm getting lots of positive feedback on my new toupee. Why, just this morning at the bank, the teller said she'd never in all her life seen hair quite like mine. I can't wait

to show it off at cousin Cindy's wedding next week.

Your mother, however, is still making fun of it. She says it's made from squirrel hair. Which is ridiculous. Because it says on the label that it's made in Guam. And I don't think they have squirrels in Guam, do they?

Got to run. Mom wants to go for a walk on the beach.

Your loving,
Daddy

To: Jausten
From: Shoptillyoudrop
Subject: Like a Dog with a Frisbee

Just back from the beach. It was very windy, and at first I thought everything was going to work out just fine. We hadn't gone two steps, when the toupee flew off Daddy's head. But he ran after it and caught it. The damn thing kept flying off, and he kept running after it and catching it. Like a dog with a frisbee. After a while, he gave up and put it in his pocket.

Of course, it got full of sand, and even though he's shaken it out a million times, sand still keeps falling out of it. So now your father has the only toupee in the world with built-in dandruff.

To: Jausten
From: DaddyO
Subject: Here's a Cute One

Here's a cute one for you, lambchop:
    What happens when you take Viagra and ExLax?
    You can't tell which way you're going!

To: DaddyO
From: Jausten

Daddy I think the punchline is supposed to be:
    You can't tell if you're coming or going.

To: Jausten
From: DaddyO

Are you sure? I thought it was funnier my way. I told it to the guys down at the clubhouse, and they couldn't stop laughing. It's amazing. Ever since I got my toupee, people find me so much more amusing than they used to. Sometimes they start laughing before I even finish my jokes.

To: Jausten
From: Shoptillyoudrop
Subject: The Most Marvelous Idea

I've just had the most marvelous idea. I know how to get rid of Daddy's toupee. It's all so simple, really.

Chapter
Five

I drove over to SueEllen's the next day, still trying to get used to the idea of Daddy with a dead squirrel on his head. I wondered what Mom's latest plan was for getting rid of it. I only hoped it didn't involve decapitation.

But all thoughts of my parents vanished when, trekking down the hallway to SueEllen's bathroom, I spotted Larkspur O'Leary coming out of one of the bedrooms. Which struck me as odd since, as far as I knew, SueEllen got her massages in her massive bathroom.

What was even more odd was Larkspur's appearance. Her face was flushed, her lipstick was smeared outside her lip line, and her long blonde hair was disheveled, as if someone had just whipped it with an egg beater. And, to top things off in the Odd Department, she was hastily buttoning her gauzy pink blouse.

Call me Sherlock, but she had all the earmarks of a woman who'd just been having sex. Or, as The Blob used to call it, Fandango.

"Hi, Larkspur!" I chirped.

She looked up from her blouse, and smiled nervously.

"Oh. Hello, Jaine," she said, quickly pulling the door shut behind her.

The woman reeked of Aramis aftershave. I knew it was Aramis because that's what The Blob used to wear when he was in the mood for Fandango. I used to try to convince him a shower would be a more effective aphrodisiac, but to no avail. Only one of the many reasons we are no longer man and wife.

Anyhow, Larkspur was reeking of the stuff.

And then I remembered: Hadn't Brad smelled of aftershave the other night? Now that I thought about it, I was almost certain it was Aramis. Was it possible that Larkspur was having a thing with Brad? Had he dashed home from school for some extracurricular activity with his mother's masseuse?

"So, Larkspur," I said. "How's it going?"

"Oh, super," she said, a nervous smile plastered on her face. "Just super." Then she looked at her watch, and pretended to be surprised. "Wow. Would you look at the time. I'm late for my next appointment. Gotta run."

And that she did, like a scared rabbit, down the hallway, her masseuse's table clunking against her thighs.

I stared at the door to the room she'd just come out of, debating whether or not to open it.

Don't be a fool, Sensible Me said. *Brad could have you fired.*

So what? said Nutcase Me. *I don't like this crummy job anyway.*

This went on for a minute or two, Sensible Me arguing with Nutcase Me. In the end, as she always does, the Nutcase won.

I opened the door. Just a few inches, enough for me to peek inside. The room, undoubtedly once a bedroom, had been converted into a home gym. Loaded with big-ticket exercise equipment. But the most important thing about the room, as far as I was concerned, was the floor to ceiling mirror covering one of the walls. Because that's where I saw the reflection of Larkspur's lover hiding behind a stairmaster, zipping his fly.

And no, it wasn't Brad.

It was his father, Hal.

Hoping Hal hadn't seen me in the

mirror, I sped down the hallway to SueEllen's bathroom. I scurried inside and was surprised to see the tub was empty. SueEllen had abandoned her perch in her marble throne, and was taking a shower. I could see the foggy outline of her fabulous body getting sprayed from all sides by multiple shower jets.

"Hi, SueEllen," I called out.

She popped her head out the shower door, her hair caught up in a terrycloth turban.

"Oh, hi, Jaine. We won't be working in the bathroom today."

If my tush could talk, it would have shouted Hallelujah.

"We're going shopping. You can take notes in the car."

I had no idea what SueEllen was going shopping for. But I knew one thing she needed: a new masseuse.

There are families in El Salvador who live in houses smaller than SueEllen's Bentley.

I sat in the front seat with her, as she navigated the hundred-thousand-dollar tub over to Heidi's school.

"I'm throwing Heidi a party for her birthday tomorrow night," SueEllen explained, "and we need to buy her a dress. By the way, I hope you can come to the party. Poor thing has no friends."

She sighed, a weak imitation of someone feeling sympathy.

"Of course," she added, "it's no surprise Heidi's so unpopular, given the way she looks."

"What's wrong with the way she looks?"

SueEllen laughed. "Have you got a couple of hours?"

"No, really, SueEllen. She looks fine to me."

SueEllen gave me the once over, taking in my unruly mop of hair, my generous thighs, and my elastic waist jeans.

"I suppose she would look fine to you."

Ouch.

"But to a kid her own age, she's got loser written all over her. Anyhow, she seems to like you. So how about it? Will you come to the party?"

"Of course. I'd be happy to."

"Marvelous, and if we're short on waitresses, you won't mind giving a hand, will you?"

Argggh. What an aggravating woman.

"Sure," I said, through gritted teeth.

"I'm glad that's settled. Let's get back to the book, shall we?"

I took out my steno pad, ready for action.

"I've got the most marvelous recipe for pot au feu," SueEllen gushed. "Actually, I got it out of a Julia Child cookbook, but we'll just change a few ingredients and no one will know the difference."

As she rattled on about Julia's pot au feu, my mind wandered back to the scene in the gym. So Hal Kingsley was having an affair with Larkspur. Frankly, I didn't blame him. Making love to SueEllen would be like mating with a piranha. I wondered if Hal had seen my reflection in the mirror. If so, would he think of an excuse to fire me? Oh, well. There was nothing I could do about it.

Several recipes later, we arrived at Beverly Hills High, where SueEllen parked in a fire zone and ran in to get Heidi, who was waiting for her at the principal's office.

"I told them it was a family emergency," SueEllen said, winking at me as she got out of the car.

Minutes later, she came sailing back out, Heidi shuffling along behind her, looking a lot like Sean Penn in *Dead Man Walking*. I guess she must have known what was in store for her.

★ ★ ★

SueEllen piloted the Bentley over to Neiman's, where she handed it over to the valet parking attendant.

"Good afternoon, Señora Kingsley," the valet greeted her.

Wow. When the parking guys at Neiman's know you by name, you're one serious shopper.

We headed up to Designer Dresses where a regal stick of a woman was waiting for us. This was Mrs. Hansen, SueEllen's longtime personal shopper. Mrs. Hansen reminded me of a black and white photo, her milky white skin and white-blonde hair in sharp contrast to her near-black lipstick and black sheath dress.

"Hello, Heidi," Mrs. Hansen cooed. "Getting ready for your big party?"

Heidi nodded miserably.

And then the torture began. It wasn't quite child abuse, but it was close. Mrs. Hansen hustled Heidi into a dressing room and proceeded to parade her out in a series of unflattering designer dresses, some of which cost more than my Corolla. All of this was accompanied by a running commentary from SueEllen, who sat in an overstuffed chair passing judgment on each fashion disaster.

81

"That'll never do," she'd say, shaking her head. "Terrible! It makes you look like a blimp." And so on.

Of course they looked terrible, I wanted to shout. These dresses were made for skinny fashionistas with serious eating disorders, not chubby fifteen year olds.

At one point, she said to Mrs. Hansen in a stage whisper that could be heard in Pomona, "She won't be so bad once she gets her nose fixed."

"Yeah," I said, "and you won't be so bad once you get your tongue ripped out."

Okay, so I didn't really say that. But I wanted to. Oh, how I wanted to. Instead, coward that I was, I just stood there, letting her chip away at Heidi's self-esteem until the poor kid was on the verge of tears. And the crazy thing was, there was nothing wrong with Heidi's nose. True, it wasn't as skinny as SueEllen's, whose nostrils were the size of sunflower seeds, but there was absolutely nothing wrong with it. Really, if I could've strangled SueEllen and gotten away with it, I would have.

Finally, SueEllen chose an unflattering blue dress with a fitted bodice that emphasized Heidi's burgeoning waistline.

"Naturally, we'll have to let out the waist," Mrs. Hansen said.

"Naturally," SueEllen echoed, rolling her eyes.

"We'll have it ready for you first thing in the morning, Mrs. Kingsley." And then, turning to Heidi, she said, "You're a mighty lucky girl to have such a generous mother."

"She's not my mother," Heidi said quietly.

"Yes," SueEllen chimed. "Don't you know? I'm the wicked stepmother."

"Ain't that the truth," were the words I wish I'd been brave enough to utter.

Heidi was back in the dressing room with a seamstress, being fitted for alterations, when SueEllen's cell phone rang. She whipped it out of her purse eagerly, as if she'd been waiting for the call.

"Oh, hi," she said, her voice suddenly softening. "Yes, I'll be there. . . . See you then."

Then she plopped her phone back in her purse, and checked out her face in a pocket mirror.

"Jaine, sweetie," she said, fluffing her hair. "I've got an important business appointment I really must keep." She handed me three twenties. "Here's cab money. Be a dear and take Heidi home, will you?"

I nodded mutely as she gathered her

things and strode off toward the escalator.

I hoped her heel got caught in one of the slats.

After a while, Heidi came out from the dressing room, looking about as perky as a Vietnam vet.

"Where's SueEllen?" she asked.

"She's gone," I said.

I could practically feel the relief flooding her body.

"She said she had a business appointment. She gave us money to take a cab home."

We took the escalator down to the first floor and were making our way past the $80 socks and $300 barrettes, when suddenly I heard someone call my name.

"Yoo hoo, Jaine!"

It was Lance, waving at us from the shoe department.

"Who's that?" Heidi asked.

"My neighbor. He works here. C'mon, let's go say hi."

I brought Heidi over and introduced her to Lance.

"Lance, this is Heidi Kingsley."

"SueEllen Kingsley's daughter?"

"Stepdaughter," we both corrected him.

"What're you guys doing here?"

"Getting a dress for Heidi," I said. "To-morrow is her birthday."

"Really?" Lance grinned. "Happy birthday, cutie pie."

How sweet. He called her cutie pie. I could have kissed him for throwing her a compliment. The poor kid probably hadn't had one in years.

Heidi blushed with pleasure.

"You gals want to try on some shoes?"

Lance knows how much I like trying on shoes I can't possibly afford.

"How about it, Heidi?" I asked. "Want to?"

She shrugged indifferently.

"Oh, come on!" Lance said. "It'll be fun."

And it was. Lance brought out box after box of outrageous shoes, and we tried them on, giggling.

"You've got beautiful feet," Lance told Heidi. "Such a slender instep." Another compliment. She soaked it up like a sponge.

After a while, two actual paying cus-tomers approached, elegant Japanese women with feet the size of Prozac's.

"Guess we'd better go," I said. Heidi and I put our shoes back in their boxes, and I hugged Lance goodbye.

"Thanks," I whispered in his ear. "You're the best."

"That's what Jim tells me," he whispered back.

"Bye, cutie," he said to Heidi, who once more blushed with pleasure.

Heidi and I headed out to Wilshire Boulevard to look for a cab, no easy feat. Finding a cab in Los Angeles is like finding a fat person in Malibu. We decided to walk over to the Beverly Wilshire Hotel, in the hopes that some cabs would be lined up out front. We hadn't gone very far when I remembered what SueEllen said about Heidi having no friends.

"Hey," I said, stopping in my tracks. "Let's not go home yet. Let's hang out for a while. Okay?"

Heidi nodded.

"Feel like a frozen yogurt?"

She nodded again.

"Well, let's go get one."

She looked out at me from under her fringe of bangs, and smiled. A beautiful smile that warmed my heart. And you know something? Lance was right. She really was a cutie pie.

It was one of those picture perfect days in Southern California, the kind of day that makes people back east kiss their storm windows goodbye and move out here, only to find themselves stuck in freeway traffic for the rest of their lives.

Heidi and I were strolling along, eating our frozen yogurts and counting the anorexics on Rodeo Drive, when Heidi said, "It wasn't really a business appointment."

"Huh?" I murmured, my attention momentarily distracted by a quatrillion dollar emerald ring in Tiffany's window.

"SueEllen didn't really have a business appointment. She's probably meeting Eduardo."

"Eduardo?"

"Her lover. He lives out in Venice. Calls himself an artist. Paints the most putrid stuff." She ran her plastic spoon along the swirls of her yogurt. "SueEllen is his sponsor. If by 'sponsor' you mean someone who boinks his brains out on a regular basis."

"How do you know for sure they're having an affair?"

"Brad caught them doing it out by the pool house. And you should see them when he comes to the house for dinner. They play footsies under the table. It's disgusting."

She took a spoonful of yogurt and shuddered.

"Does your father know?"

"I'm not sure," she said. "But I think Daddy's having an affair, too. With Larkspur."

SueEllen and Hal were quite the couple, weren't they? They reminded me of the joke about the guy whose wife had been cheating on him for years, and didn't find out about it until his mistress finally told him.

"I hope Daddy divorces SueEllen and marries Larkspur. She's a ditz, but at least she's nicer than SueEllen."

Hell, Attila the Hun would be nicer than SueEllen.

"I knew SueEllen was trouble the first time we met. She and Daddy took us to Disneyland. She spent the whole ride down to Anaheim rubbing Daddy's thigh. Brad and I could see it from the back seat of the car, and she knew we could see it. It was like she was telling us, *he's mine and there's nothing you can do about it.*"

She paused to eat another spoonful of her yogurt. I'd long since finished mine and was scraping the dish for the soupy stuff.

"Daddy knew we didn't like her, so he

88

married her while Brad and I were away at summer camp. We never even knew about it until we came home. There she was, standing at the front door, smiling that bitchy smile of hers. And then, when I went upstairs and saw what she did to my room, I hated her more than ever."

"What did she do?"

She shook her head, still miserable at the memory of what happened.

"You see, the thing is, I really loved my room. The ceiling was sky blue with clouds painted all over it. My mom painted it, before I was born. After my mom died, I'd lay in bed at night and look up at the ceiling, and it was like my mom was there in the room with me. It was the one thing I had left of her. And SueEllen took it away. While I was gone, she'd painted over it. A hideous hot pink. She said she saw a picture of a room just like it in *Vogue*."

"What a bitch," I blurted out.

"When she asked me how I liked it, I told her the truth. That I hated it. And ever since then, she's treated me like crap. I can't wait till I'm eighteen and go away to college."

By now we'd walked the length of Rodeo Drive, past the Hermès scarves and the

Gucci handbags and the Louis Vuitton luggage.

"Heidi," I said, "I hope you don't mind my asking, but what happened to your mom?"

"Cancer. She died when I was ten."

"Oh, honey. I'm so sorry."

Her eyes welled with tears.

"Why couldn't SueEllen be the one who got cancer?"

I couldn't think of a thing to say to take away the pain, so I squeezed her hand, and hoped it would comfort her.

"What would you like to do next?" I asked.

"It doesn't matter," she said, shrugging.

"Sure it does," I insisted. "We're going to have fun if it kills us."

She managed a weak smile.

"Okay, then," she said. "Let's go to the Museum of Television and Radio. It's right around the corner. I go there all the time after school."

We tossed our empty yogurt dishes into a trash can and headed around the corner to the Museum of Television and Radio. A stark white minimalist building, the museum has an amazing collection of vintage TV and radio shows. You pick out the show you want, and watch it on your own private console.

For the next few hours Heidi and I sat watching TV shows of yesteryear. I whiled away the time with two of my comedy favorites, Lucy and Alf. Heidi's choices proved to be very interesting: *My Little Margie* and *Bachelor Father*.

Bachelor Father is a show about an orphaned teenage girl living with her unmarried uncle. *My Little Margie* is about a young woman living with her widowed father. Not a stepmom in sight.

You didn't have to be Sigmund Freud to figure out that Heidi would have given anything to be like these girls and have her father all to herself.

Chapter Six

"First kick them in the groin. If that doesn't work, try gouging out their eyes."

Kandi was sitting across from me at Paco's Tacos, sipping a margarita and plying me with self-defense tips. Ever since she started her martial arts class, she'd morphed into an encyclopedia of dire warnings.

"If you're ever thrown into the trunk of a car, kick out a back tail light and stick your arm out the hole and wave like crazy."

"The next time I'm thrown into the trunk of a car, I'll do just that," I said, digging in to my beef burrito.

"It could happen," she warned.

"I know. And if it does, I'll do it. I promise."

Her eyes lit up with the fervor of the recently converted.

"I can't tell you how much I'm learning from this class."

"I think you already have. Thanks to you, I now know twelve different ways to maim a guy." I took a chip and dipped it into my refried beans. "So what's happening with your instructor?"

"Matt," she sighed, her chin resting in her hand. "Darling Matt."

"Has Darling Matt asked you out yet?"

"Yep," she grinned. "Dinner at the beach. This Saturday."

"That's great," I said, trying to sound like I meant it. Somehow I couldn't picture Kandi hooking up with a guy who chopped wood with his fist.

"And what about you?" she asked. "Have you heard from Ted Lawson?"

"Tommy the Termite? He called the other night and asked me out to dinner."

"I assume you were a fool and turned him down."

"No, as a matter of fact, I was a fool and said yes."

"Oh, honey. That's wonderful!" Kandi beamed.

Then her perfectly plucked brows furrowed.

"What are you going to wear?"

"I don't know."

"What do you mean, you don't know?"

"I'm not seeing him until the end of the week. I haven't even thought about it."

"That's just your trouble, Jaine. You

should be thinking about it. You've got to make a good first impression."

"How about I kick him in the groin? That ought to impress him."

"Whatever you do," she said, ignoring my feeble attempt at sarcasm, "don't wear elastic waist pants. It's so Trailer Park."

"But they're comfortable," I whined.

"Tough," she said, checking out her reflection in her knife. "You've got to suffer for beauty."

"I don't want to suffer for beauty. The only thing I'm willing to suffer for is a hot fudge sundae."

"Which reminds me, do you really think you should be eating that burrito? It has at least a gazillion calories."

"Hey," I said, clutching my plate, "if I wanted to be nagged to death, I'd move to Florida and live with my parents."

"Sorry. I only want to see you happy."

"If you really want to see me happy, you'll order me another margarita. And a change of subject might be nice."

"Okay," she said. "I'll change the subject. Did you know you're seven times more likely to be attacked in a stairwell than in an elevator?"

And so it went, a litany of warnings that didn't stop, not even when we went to get our cars in the parking lot.

"Remember. If you're parked next to a van, always enter your car from the passenger door. Most serial killers attack their victim by pulling the woman into their van while she's trying to get into her car."

"Thanks for a fun evening," I said, escaping into my car.

The last thing I heard as I drove out the lot was Kandi shouting: "If someone is following you, drive straight to the nearest police station!"

I don't mind admitting I was a tad nervous driving back to Beverly Hills. After an evening of Kandi's lurid self-defense tips, I imagined I saw homicidal maniacs at every stop light.

Finally, I made it home. Just my luck, there were no parking spots outside my duplex so I had to park down at the end of the street and walk back. I was halfway home when I started hearing footsteps behind me. Too frightened to turn around, I quickened my pace. By the time I got to my duplex I was practically sprinting. I turned up the path to my apartment. The footsteps were right behind me.

Omigod. Kandi was right. Homicidal maniacs *were* lurking at every corner. I'd been a fool not to take her seriously.

"Jaine?"

I whirled around to face my assailant.

Thank heavens, it was only Lance.

"I thought it was you, Jaine, but I wasn't sure."

"Lance! I thought you were a sex pervert about to attack me."

"Sorry to disappoint you, hon. But I'm saving all my sexual perversions for Jim. Are you okay?"

"I'll be fine as soon as my heart starts beating again."

"Are you sure?"

"I'm fine. Really."

After assuring Lance I wasn't on the verge of a coronary, we said goodnight and I let myself into my apartment. I fed Prozac her midnight snack of minced mackerel guts, then brushed and flossed my teeth and climbed into bed. (Okay, so I didn't floss, but I promise I will tomorrow.)

I turned on the TV and surfed for a while, but I couldn't concentrate. I couldn't stop thinking about SueEllen and how badly she treated Heidi. I thought about how she'd humiliated her at dinner, refusing to let her eat dessert, and making her sit there while she oohed and aahed about how delicious it was. I thought about her cruel nose job crack at Neiman's. And finally, I thought about how she'd repainted Heidi's bedroom, destroying her one last connection to her mom.

I thought about all this, and I wanted to kill her.

Little did I know that someone else was about to beat me to it.

Chapter
Seven

It was the night of Heidi's birthday party, and as I drove my Corolla up the Kingsleys' circular driveway, I felt like Cinderella showing up at the ball in a bruised pumpkin. Mine was the only non-luxury car for miles around. In fact, the driveway bore a striking resemblance to a Mercedes dealership.

I checked my reflection in my rear view mirror. I'd spent a good twenty minutes blowing out the curls in my hair, and I was pleased to see they were still being held at bay. I got out of the car, smoothing my silk pantsuit. Kandi would have been disappointed to know that the pants had an elastic waist, but it was hidden under a flowing jacket. Actually, it was a very flattering outfit; if I held in my stomach and stopped breathing, I could maybe pass for a size 8.

A stunning actor/valet parker came trotting to my side.

"You with the catering staff?" he said, eyeing my Corolla as if it were a waterbug. "If so, you've got to park down the street."

"No," I huffed, with all the dignity I could muster. "I'm a guest."

At least I hoped I was. For all I knew, SueEllen would be whisking me out of my pantsuit and into a waitress's uniform.

I watched as the valet took my car and drove off down the driveway, no doubt to park it on another street, perhaps in another town, so as not to contaminate the Mercedes.

An attractive blond maid greeted me at the door. Where was Conchi? Probably stuck in the kitchen, slaving over a recipe stolen from Julia Child. The blonde welcomed me to Casa Kingsley and ushered me into the cavernous living room. Even with thirty or so guests and a bunch of actor/waitpersons milling around, the room still looked huge.

"Jaine, sweetie!"

SueEllen came sashaying over in skin tight black leather slacks and matching bustier. The Marquis de Sade meets Auntie Mame. Thankfully, she made no mention of my being needed in the kitchen. It looked like I wasn't assigned to KP duty, after all.

"How nice you could come!" she cooed.

"And what a super outfit. It hides your monster thighs."

Okay, so she didn't make the thigh crack, but that's what she was thinking.

"Come say hello to the birthday girl," she said, grabbing my elbow and steering me over to where Heidi stood in her unflattering blue dress, eating a stuffed mushroom. I glanced around the room, looking for kids Heidi's age, but I didn't see any. Clearly, my job was to be Heidi's friend for the night. A job I was more than happy to accept.

"I wouldn't eat any more of those if I were you," SueEllen said, eyeing the hors d'oeuvre in Heidi's hand. "You're practically splitting your seams as it is."

And with that, she took off to chat up some people far more important than us. Heidi made a face behind her back, and popped the rest of the mushroom in her mouth.

"These are great," she said. "They're stuffed with crab. Want one?"

"Sure."

Heidi flagged down Conchi who was circulating a platter of mushrooms, the only Hispanic among the perky caterer's assistants.

"Hey, Conchi," I said. "How's it going?"

"Muy bueno, Miss Jaine," she said shyly, handing me a linen cocktail napkin. How impressive. My guests are lucky to get paper napkins left over from my last McDonald's order. Heidi and I each plucked a mushroom from the platter, and Conchi headed off to make the rounds of the room.

"These are fabulous," I said, the crab literally melting in my mouth.

"SueEllen claims it's an old family recipe, but she got it from Emeril Lagasse's cookbook. Oh, rats. She's giving me the evil eye."

SueEllen had momentarily diverted attention from her A-List guests and was glaring at Heidi. Heidi popped the mushroom in her mouth defiantly.

"I got you something for your birthday," I said, reaching into my purse for the present I'd picked up for her earlier that day.

"Gee, thanks, Jaine."

She ripped open the package eagerly.

"A book! By P. G. Wodehouse. How did you know I love P. G. Wodehouse?"

"I saw you reading one of his books the day we met."

"Oh, Jaine. Thank you so much!"

Then I reached out and hugged her. I

had a feeling she didn't get many hugs at Casa Kingsley.

"Happy birthday, kiddo."

"It is, now that you're here," she said, melting my heart.

"Oh, look," she whispered. "There's Eduardo, SueEllen's lover."

"Where?"

"Over there. By the fireplace."

Hubba hubba. The guy was a stunner. With his tight bod, smoldering eyes, and slicked-back hair, he looked like he just stepped out of a Calvin Klein underwear ad. He stood leaning against the fireplace, in a Hawaiian print shirt and pleated linen trousers, talking to a young blonde with yet another perfect body. Good heavens, wasn't there anybody at this party aside from Heidi and me with a waist bigger than Barbie's?

"Who's the girl he's talking to?"

"That's Amber. Brad's girlfriend."

I remembered what Brad said the other night about having sex on the den carpet. I had no trouble whatsoever picturing this tootsie getting carpet burns on her fanny.

"Where's Brad?"

"At the bar."

I looked over to where Brad was standing at a makeshift bar set up in the corner of the room, tapping his foot impatiently while the bartender fixed him a drink.

"He sure doesn't look like a happy camper," I said.

"Oh, Brad's pissed because SueEllen convinced Daddy not to buy him a Ferrari. He's getting a Beemer instead."

Poor darling. My heart bled for him.

"I told Brad she'd never let Daddy buy the Ferrari, but he didn't believe me. And now he's furious."

And indeed, Brad looked like he was barely containing himself as he glowered at the slow moving bartender.

"Heidi, sweetheart. Come say hello to the Millers."

Hal was standing at our side, craggy and casual in a turtleneck and jeans. He looked me straight in the eye, not the least bit uncomfortable. Not like a man who'd recently been caught zipping his fly after sex. Which meant he probably hadn't seen me spying on him.

But wouldn't Larkspur have told him about our encounter in the hallway? And if so, shouldn't he have been worried that I might suspect something and spill the beans to SueEllen? Oh, well. Maybe he just didn't care. He was a surgeon, after all. After years of sucking fat out of women's thighs, the guy probably had nerves of steel.

"You don't mind my borrowing Heidi, do you, Jaine?"

"No, of course not."

I was happy that somebody at Heidi's birthday party actually wanted to talk to her.

Hal led her over to a middle-aged couple eating baby lamb chops.

God, they were gorgeous. Not the couple — the lamb chops. I decided to circulate and see if I could find some. I made the rounds of the room, past the social string beans sipping their chardonnay and nibbling their hors d'oeuvres. And when I say nibbling I mean nibbling. It took some of those anorexics five bites to finish a one-inch shrimp puff.

At last I tracked down the lamb chops. The attractive blonde who'd greeted me at the front door was carrying a platter full of the little darlings.

"Hi," I said. "I've been looking all over for these. May I?"

"Of course," she said, handing me a napkin.

I plucked one off the tray, and took a bite.

"Hmmm. Divine."

"Want another?" she grinned. "For the road?"

"Don't mind if I do."

I took one more (okay, two more) and headed over to the bar to get myself some wine.

Brad was still at the bar, slugging down his drink, his hot young girlfriend at his side. The lovely Amber looked bored. She'd seemed a lot more animated when she was talking to Eduardo.

"Hi, Brad." I flashed him a smile, but he just stared at me blankly. The guy clearly had no idea who I was. Or if he did know, he didn't care.

"I'm Jaine Austen, SueEllen's writer."

"Whatever."

He took another slug of his drink and muttered: "That bitch. She screwed me out of my Ferrari. I hope she chokes on one of her own hors d'oeuvres."

I assumed that the bitch in question was SueEllen.

Amber wrinkled her perfect nose in annoyance. "Brad, cool it on the booze, will you? You're getting obnoxious."

Getting? I'd say he'd hit obnoxious three drinks ago.

I scooted away as soon as I got my wine. Something told me Brad wasn't in the mood for my company. And neither was anybody else. I wandered around with a friendly smile on my face, but aside from Heidi and the blonde waitress with the lamb chops, nobody at the party seemed the least bit interested in talking to me.

Heidi was still busy chatting with the middle-aged couple, so I decided to head outside to the terrace and gnaw on my lamb chops without any Emily Post types giving me dirty looks. I stepped out through a pair of magnificent French doors onto a magnificent terrace, under a magnificent moon, no doubt ordered by SueEllen especially for the occasion.

I plopped down onto a chaise lounge with a cushion as thick as a mattress, and tasted the chardonnay. Lovely. No Screw Top Specials at Casa Kingsley. Then I sat back and gnawed at my lamb chops until the bones were white. Utter heaven.

Eventually my bliss was interrupted by the sound of laughter. A slim young Armani couple joined me on the terrace, waving their wine glasses, giggling over some private joke. They caught sight of me on the chaise and quickly looked away, saying nothing. These two were clearly not interested in making friends. They continued whispering and giggling until I felt like an unwanted chaperone at a high school prom.

I looked inside and saw Heidi, now busily chatting with another couple. I had no real desire to go back to the party, so I grabbed the remains of my lamb chops and started strolling the grounds.

The moon was full and the grass was like velvet under my feet. I headed towards the back of the house where, for the first time, I saw the Kingsleys' pool. A lovely turquoise thing, it glittered in the moonlight like a Home Shopping Club aquamarine ring.

Just beyond the pool was a charming cottage, obviously the pool house. I decided to walk over and check it out. I made my way past some designer deck chairs to the cottage door, which was partially open. I heard voices coming from inside.

"For God's sake, SueEllen," a man was saying, panic in his voice. "It was just a one-time indiscretion."

For the second time in two days, I was tempted to peek in a forbidden door to see who SueEllen was talking to. But this time, Sensible Me won out. The prospect of being spotted by SueEllen was too scary to risk. I settled for eavesdropping.

"You're not going to tell people about it,

are you?" the man pleaded.

"Of course I am," SueEllen said, breezily.

"But you'll ruin my career," the man said, his voice rising a full octave with fear.

"You think I care about your career now? After what I know?"

"I swear, SueEllen. It won't happen again."

"Forget it, Eduardo." Okay, so now I knew who she was talking to. "You're history in this town. You'll be lucky to get a job drawing caricatures on the Santa Monica Pier."

Then I heard the clack of her heels on the wood floor.

"SueEllen, wait! Don't go."

Damn. She was on her way out the door, and I was standing there in full view, still clutching my lamb chop bones. I looked around for a place to hide. Nothing. Nada. Not a bush in sight. Just a few potted palms, dotted among the deck chairs. I dashed behind one of them, praying that SueEllen wouldn't spot me. It wouldn't have been hard to do. It was like trying to hide behind a phone pole. I would've given anything at that moment to be one of SueEllen's ninety-eight-pound bulimic buddies.

SueEllen came sailing out the door, looking a lot like a Sunset Boulevard dominatrix in her black leather ensemble. Thankfully, she didn't even glance my way. A miserable Eduardo followed in her wake.

"SueEllen! Please!" he called after her. "Can't we talk this over?"

But she kept on walking, ignoring him.

He looked at her retreating figure, and raked his fingers through his hair so roughly I thought he'd yank it out. Then slowly he started trudging back to the party.

I waited till he was gone and crept out from my hiding place. Then I tossed my lamb chop bones into one of the potted palms and headed back to the party, wondering exactly what kind of indiscretion Eduardo had committed.

Dinner was served buffet style in the dining room. The dining table was laden with an impressive array of gourmet dishes handed down from Aunt Melanie and Julia Child. Needless to say, there wasn't a plastic fork in sight. In fact, the sterling silver was so heavy, a person could get carpal tunnel syndrome just lifting it. Heidi and I stood on line together, and loaded our plates with crab cakes, veal marsala, and crispy roasted new potatoes.

Heidi was just reaching for a roll when SueEllen crept up behind her.

"Is that roll really necessary, darling?"

Heidi looked her straight in the eye.

"Yep," she said, and tossed it onto her plate.

Score one for Heidi.

SueEllen seethed.

"Whatever you say, hon." Her smile was as sharp as a Ginsu knife.

We all took our plates back into the living room and sat around in chummy clumps.

The dinner dynamics were interesting, to put it mildly.

Heidi and I nabbed seats on one of several overstuffed sofas. Brad sat across from us on a matching sofa, ignoring his food and glaring at SueEllen. Amber, sitting between Brad and Eduardo, was ignoring Brad and flirting with Eduardo. But Eduardo was oblivious to her charms, barely touching his food, and shooting imploring looks at SueEllen. SueEllen was perched on the arm of Hal's chair, also ignoring her food, and rubbing her husband's neck seductively. Perhaps she planned on being a faithful wife for a bit, to while away the time between lovers.

I'm happy to report that Heidi seemed to be having a good time. SueEllen wouldn't dare be her ugly self in front of all these people, some of whom were, no doubt, very influential in town. So, for the duration of the evening, Heidi was safe.

At least, that's what I thought. Until one of the guests, during a lull in the conversation, turned to me, and said, "And what do you do, Ms. Austen?"

Before I could reply, SueEllen piped up: "Jaine's my secretary. She's taking dictation for my book. Isn't that right, Jaine, dear?"

Clearly, she didn't want anyone to know she was using a ghostwriter.

I smiled and muttered a noncommittal *Hmmm.*

"She's amazing, isn't she?" Heidi whispered. "God forbid she should give anybody credit for anything."

"It's okay," I lied. "I don't mind."

"Yeah, well, I do." Then she cleared her throat, and said, "Actually, Jaine's a writer. She's ghostwriting SueEllen's book."

A hush fell over the room.

Everyone looked at SueEllen to see what she would say.

"Well, yes," she said, smiling a brittle smile, "Jaine is helping me just a tad with

111

the writing. And doing a marvelous job, I might add. In fact, when I'm through with this book, I think I may write another. A diet book for fat teenagers."

Accent on the *fat.*

Oh, Christ. The gloves were off. To hell with the dinner guests. SueEllen was out for blood.

I looked over at Heidi, who was blushing furiously. No one (except possibly Brad, who was practically unconscious with booze) could have missed SueEllen's dig.

And it was at that unfortunate moment that Conchi chose to wheel in Heidi's birthday cake, a towering confection with sixteen candles and *Happy Birthday, Heidi,* emblazoned across the pink icing.

"And look what's here," SueEllen said. "Heidi's birthday cake! But what will the rest of us be eating, Conchi?"

"That's enough, SueEllen," Hal said, his jaw clenched.

"Oh, Heidi doesn't mind a little kidding, do you, sweetie?"

Heidi just sat there, staring down at her hands.

Then somebody started singing *Happy Birthday.* Everyone joined in, eager to fill the painful silence.

When we were all through singing,

someone shouted, "Make a wish."

"Yes," everybody chorused. "Make a wish."

But before Heidi could make her wish, SueEllen piped up:

"Better wish for a new nose."

It was as if Heidi were frozen in her chair, the way she kept sitting there, eyes lowered, not moving a muscle. Oh, God, I prayed. Please don't let her cry. Not in front of all these people.

But Heidi didn't cry. At last, she raised her face and was surprisingly dry-eyed.

"No, SueEllen," she said. "That's not my wish. Here's my wish: I wish you were dead. Too bad I said it out loud. Now it probably won't come true."

Then she blew out the candles, every damn one of them, and walked out of the room.

For once in her life, SueEllen Kingsley was speechless.

For once in *my* life, I didn't stick around for birthday cake.

I hurried out into the foyer, looking for Heidi, but she was nowhere in sight. I headed upstairs, figuring she'd gone to her room. I had no idea where Heidi's bedroom was, so I ran down the hallway opening doors at random. At last I found a room painted a hideous hot pink. Heidi was lying on her bed in her bra and panties, staring up at the ceiling, perhaps remembering the fluffy clouds her mother had once painted for her. She'd taken off her ugly party dress and tossed it carelessly on the floor.

"I wish I had a fireplace so I could burn that thing."

"Heidi, are you okay?"

"I'm fine," she said, sitting up.

And she was. I'd expected to find her bawling her eyes out, but she was surprisingly calm. I sat down at the edge of her bed, and smoothed her bangs away from her face.

"I've made up my mind," she said. "I won't let SueEllen hurt me any more. I'm not scared of her. Or of Daddy, either. I don't care what they do to me. They can send me away to boarding school. In fact, I hope they do."

"I'd hate to see you go, but I think you'd be happier away from SueEllen."

Heidi flopped back onto her pillow and sighed.

"Oh, Jaine, why couldn't Daddy have married someone like you?"

"Because your daddy thinks with his penis, that's why."

Of course, I didn't really say that. What I said was, "If I'm ever a mother, I hope my daughter turns out just like you."

Then I kissed her on her forehead.

"It's late. I'd better be going."

I started for the door when she called to me.

"Jaine."

"Yes?"

"I don't really wish SueEllen was dead."

"I know you don't."

"I just wish she was fat and broke and living in Tijuana."

Yep, Heidi was my kind of daughter, all right.

Downstairs, the party was breaking up. People were suddenly remembering baby-sitters they had to pay and early morning appointments they had to get up for. Anything to make their escape.

SueEllen was busy air-kissing them all goodbye, promising to "do lunch," floating from one to the other as if her party hadn't just imploded into a million pieces.

I hurried out the door, hoping to beat the valet rush. But I was too late. An anxious knot of guests were already standing around waiting for their cars.

I nabbed a valet and said, "Just give me

my keys. I can get my car myself. White Corolla."

I slipped him two bucks, and he tossed me my keys.

"It's that way," he said, pointing vaguely down the street.

I found my car five blocks away, among a string of economy cars, obviously in the "hired hands" parking section.

Driving home that night, I made up my mind to quit my job. I didn't care how much SueEllen was paying me. She was a dreadful woman and my tush and I simply didn't want to work for her any more. I'd hand in my resignation tomorrow.

When I got back to the apartment, I broke the news to Prozac.

"It looks like we're not going to be rich, after all, lovebug."

Prozac was so upset, she almost looked up from her genitals.

YOU'VE GOT MAIL!

To: Jausten
From: DaddyO
Subject: Brace Yourself!

Brace yourself for a shock, pumpkin. My

116

toupee is missing. And I know who took it. Your mother. She claims she has no idea where it is, but I wasn't born yesterday. It didn't just get up and walk out of the house, did it?

I've looked high and low, but it's not here. I guess your mother couldn't stand the fact that other women found me so attractive in it.

I'm not sure I'll ever be able to forgive her for this act of treachery.

Daddy

To: Jausten
From: Shoptillyoudrop
Subject: Heavenly Day!

Oh, heavenly day! I got rid of the wig! It was so simple, really. I just waited till Daddy was asleep and I brought it out to the garbage. I buried it beneath Taffy's cat food cans. He'll never think to look for it there.

Now I can enjoy myself at cousin Cindy's wedding! If only I could remember who Charleton McAfee is. Maybe Earlene's first husband? But I could've sworn his name was Lester. Besides, I thought Lester had run out on poor Earlene years ago. The way I heard it, he went to buy a box of Milk Duds at the movies, and was never seen again. Oh, well. I guess I'll just have to wait till the wedding to find out who Mr. McAfee is.

By the way, honey, I bought the most adorable polyester charmeuse pants suit from the shopping channel. It's a genuine Georgie O. Armani. Who says the shopping channel doesn't have famous designers?

Well, we're off to play Bingo at the clubhouse.

All my love to you and Prilosec,
Mom

To: Jausten
From: DaddyO
Subject: Not my fault!

I just want to go on record: What happened at the clubhouse was NOT my fault!

To: Jausten
From: Shoptillyoudrop
Subject: You won't believe what just happened!

Oh, dear. You won't believe what just happened at the clubhouse. Daddy saw a man at the bingo table with a thick head of hair. And for some insane reason, Daddy was convinced it was his toupee.

And right there in the middle of Bingo, he got up and accused this perfectly lovely man of stealing his toupee! And if that wasn't bad enough, he tried to grab it from his head. Of course, the man wasn't wearing a toupee, and Daddy wound up yanking out a clump of this poor man's hair. It was very painful, I'm sure.

The absolute worst thing is that the man turned out to be Tampa Vista's new social director. So now Daddy's been banned from the clubhouse for the next six months.

To: Jausten
From: DaddyO
Subject: Bingo

I never liked that clubhouse, anyhow. I think the bingo games are fixed.

Chapter
Eight

"I've worked for a lot of sleazeballs in my life, SueEllen, but you hit a new low on the sleaze-o-meter. Effective immediately, I quit."

Nice speech, isn't it? I spent the next morning in front of the mirror rehearsing it, along with a few other choice zingers. (*I'm sickened by the way you mistreat Heidi, and I intend to file a complaint about you with county social services. From now on, you can turn on your own damned hot water.* And my personal fave: *The last time I saw boobs like yours was at a volleyball game.*)

By the time I got to work, I'd mentally tried and convicted SueEllen of child (and writer) abuse, and had her sharing a jail cell with a gal named Duke.

Of course, SueEllen wasn't the only person on my mind that morning. There was also Daddy and that ridiculous toupee of his. I didn't blame Mom one bit for tossing it in the trash, especially after that scene at the clubhouse. It was just like

Daddy to pull a stranger's hair in the middle of a bingo game. Just like the time he punched out "the burglar" he caught on our front steps. It turned out the man was a Jehovah's Witness who, after he regained consciousness, sued Daddy for $1,200 in small claims court and won.

Life with Daddy sure wasn't easy, I thought, as I drove up the Kingsleys' driveway.

I parked my Corolla next to SueEllen's Bentley and headed for the front door. I rang the bell, but nobody answered. I rang it again. Still no answer. That was strange. Even if nobody else was home, why wasn't SueEllen letting me in with her bathtub intercom?

Just when I was about to give up and turn away, Heidi opened the door, a Walkman headset hanging from her neck.

"I thought I heard the doorbell, but I wasn't sure. Come on in."

I followed her inside and up the stairs.

"What're you doing home from school?"

I hoped SueEllen hadn't grounded her for life.

"Ugh," she groaned. "Student elections. Couldn't bear listening to the campaign speeches so I cut out early."

"How's everything going?" I asked, wondering if there'd been any ugly aftermath of the Birthday Cake Affair.

"Fine. This morning at breakfast, SueEllen said I couldn't have any pancakes. So I went into the kitchen and got them myself. SueEllen had a cow, but for once, Daddy stuck up for me and told her to let me eat 'the goddam pancakes.' "

"Good for you."

"I would've never been able to do it without you, Jaine."

"Me?"

"The other night, when you said you weren't going to eat dessert if I couldn't have any, SueEllen was really mad. But you didn't care. You stood up to her. Not many people do. I figured if you could do it, I could, too. You gave me the courage to stick up for myself."

Then we launched into one of those mushy hugs that were becoming part of our repertoire.

"Look, Heidi. There's something I've got to tell you. I'm quitting. You said nobody ever lasted with SueEllen more than a week. And you were right. She's impossible."

Heidi blanched. "But you can't quit. When will I see you?"

"We can meet after school."

"What happens when you get another job?"

She had me there.

"Can't you stay a little while longer, until I get used to this 'stick up for myself' thing?"

The thought of one more day on that damn toilet bowl made me cringe, but she looked so vulnerable, I couldn't say no.

"Okay," I sighed. "But just for a few more weeks."

As it turned out, I didn't even have to stay a few more hours. Because when I walked into the bathroom to report for work, the first thing I saw was SueEllen floating face down in the bathtub.

"SueEllen?" I called out, hoping maybe she was doing some new age water aerobics.

But she didn't answer. Dead people rarely do.

At first I thought it was an accident; maybe SueEllen slipped in the tub. But then I saw something floating alongside SueEllen's loofa sponge and triple-milled French soap: A hair dryer. Plugged in to an electrical outlet.

Good Lord. SueEllen had been electrocuted!

I managed to keep my cool for a whole three and a half seconds. After which I went screaming down the hallway like an extra in *Nightmare on Elm Street*.

Heidi hurried out from her room, her Walkman still hanging from her neck.

"Jaine, what's wrong?"

"SueEllen," I managed to gasp. "She's dead. Electrocuted in the bathtub with a hair dryer."

"Oh, my God." Heidi's eyes widened with disbelief.

"I think it was murder."

"Murder? Are you sure?"

"SueEllen would never have been stupid enough to use a hair dryer in a tub full of water. Besides, her vanity table was clear across the room. She would have dried her hair over there."

Someone else tossed that dryer in the tub. Of that I was certain.

"Let's go downstairs," I said, wanting to put at least a staircase between me and SueEllen's corpse, "and call the cops."

A half-hour later, the place was swarming with Beverly Hills cops. Who were, I couldn't help noticing, an unusually attractive bunch. Clean cut and strong jawed, they looked like Dudley Do-Rights with suntans. Leave it to Beverly Hills to hire beautiful cops to match the beautiful houses.

The detective who questioned me bore a striking resemblance to Clint Eastwood. Lieutenant Jonathan Webb was tall and craggy, with a cleft in his chin the size of a dime. He asked me a bunch of questions about what time I'd shown up and how I knew the deceased, and if I'd seen anyone suspicious entering or leaving the premises. As I answered him, I kept staring at the cleft in his chin, wondering how he shaved around it. It's funny what you think about when you've just seen a dead body in a bathtub.

Finally, when I'd answered all his questions and assured him I had no idea who could've possibly tossed a hair dryer in SueEllen's tub, he let me go.

On my way out I saw Heidi huddled with Hal and Brad in the living room. Brad sat hunched over with his chin resting on his clasped hands, tapping his feet in a nervous staccato. Hal stared straight ahead, his face an impassive mask. I had no idea what he was thinking. He could've been overcome with grief, or simply wondering what to order for dinner.

Heidi sat between them, dazed with disbelief. I tried to make eye contact, but she didn't see me. I figured I'd call her later, once she had a chance to let the news sink in. Meanwhile, I wanted to get the hell out of there.

Which is exactly what I did. I got in my Corolla and raced home, if you consider inching along at ten miles an hour in rush hour traffic "racing."

Normally in times of stress I head straight for the bathtub. But after what I'd just seen, the very thought of a bath sent chills down my spine. Instead, I opted for a nice relaxing shower. Followed by an even more relaxing glass of chardonnay.

I stayed in the shower for at least twenty minutes, letting the hot water cascade down my back until my muscles were the consistency of tapioca pudding. Then I padded out to the kitchen in my ratty chenille robe and poured myself that much needed glass of wine. The whole idea of SueEllen electrocuted with her own hair dryer gave me the creeps. Sure, she was a dreadful woman, but she didn't deserve to die. Not like that, anyway.

I sat down on my sofa and sipped (okay, gulped) my wine, trying to erase the image of SueEllen's perfect tush bobbing in the water next to the dryer. I couldn't help thinking about the irony of it all — that a woman like SueEllen Kingsley, obsessed with looking beautiful, had been murdered with a deadly grooming aid.

Prozac, sensing my distress and knowing how much I needed her comforting presence, began yowling for her dinner.

As I trudged back to the kitchen to open a can of gourmet beef innards, I realized I was hungry, too. I hadn't had a thing to eat all day except six Altoids and a Whopper I'd picked up on my way over to Sue-Ellen's. I rummaged through the kitchen drawer where I dump all the take-out restaurant menus that are left on my doorstep. I found one for Sir Speedy Pizza — "The Fastest Pizza in the West."

I called Sir Speedy, and ordered a medium pizza with mushroom and pepperoni. Prozac looked up from her beef innards and shot me a look.

"And throw in a few anchovies."

Prozac purred in approval and went back to her dinner.

The folks at Sir Speedy promised the pizza would be at my doorstep, piping hot, in thirty minutes or less. I hung up and poured myself some more wine to tide me over until it showed up. Then I headed for the bedroom. I figured I'd soothe my frazzled nerves with some TV. Of course, wouldn't you know, the first thing I saw when I turned on the television was the bathtub scene from *Fatal Attraction*, where Glenn Close gets stabbed to death in the tub. I zapped around for a while, past Lucy and Larry King and a painful looking Pilates contraption on QVC. I was just getting comfortable watching Emeril Lagasse do obscene things to a catfish, when the doorbell rang.

Wow. It was only fifteen minutes since I'd called Sir Speedy. That *was* fast. I'd have to give the delivery kid a big tip. I grabbed my wallet, and opened the door.

But it wasn't Sir Speedy.

It was Lance.

"I just heard the news on the radio. They said SueEllen Kingsley was murdered in her tub, and that a freelance writer discovered the body. Was that you?"

I nodded wearily.

"Tell me everything!"

"There's not much to tell. I showed up for work and found her dead in the tub."

"That must've been awful! You shouldn't be alone at a time like this."

He was probably right.

"Actually, I just ordered a pizza. Why don't you stay and have dinner with me?"

"Fine. Just let me call Jim and cancel."

"You have a date?"

"It's nothing. Jim won't mind."

"No, no. Don't cancel."

"Are you sure? It's no problem. So what if I'm madly in love with the guy and can't stand to be apart for him for more than fifteen minutes at a stretch?"

Okay, so he didn't say the part about being madly in love with Jim, but I knew that's what he was thinking.

"I'll be fine," I assured him.

"Okay," he said, trying to hide his relief. "We'll talk later." And then he dashed off.

I shuffled back to the TV and was watching Emeril slosh some shrimp into a vat of bubbling fat, when the phone rang.

"Omigod," said Kandi. "I just heard the news. Are you okay?"

"I'm fine," I lied. "Want to come over for pizza?"

"Oh, gee, I wish I could, but we're working late tonight. The actress who plays Maggie the Maggot just checked herself into Betty Ford, and we have to write her out of the script. Are you sure you're going to be okay?"

"I'll be fine. The pizza will calm me down."

And it's true. I happen to believe that pizza is one of nature's most effective sedatives. Something in the cheese, I think.

"Well, if you need anything, just call me at the studio."

I assured her I would, and went back to the TV. By now, Emeril had fished the shrimp out of the fryer. Gad, they looked good. Now I was hungrier than ever. Where the heck was that pizza? And at that very moment the doorbell rang. Exactly a half hour after I'd ordered it. My hero Sir Speedy had lived up to his word. I raced to the door, eager to sink my teeth in a wad of gooey cheese.

But it wasn't Sir Speedy.

It was Heidi. Standing on my doorstep with a suitcase.

"Oh, Jaine," she wailed. "The cops think I killed SueEllen."

I took her suitcase and ushered her inside.

"How on earth did you get here?"

"I took a cab. I was so scared, I didn't want to be alone."

"Alone? But what about your dad and your brother? Aren't they home?"

"Yes," she said. "They're home."

She looked up at me from under her fringe of bangs. Her eyes were red from crying, and at that moment, I realized how very much alone she was in that big house of hers.

"Can I stay with you tonight?"

"Of course you can, honey. Make yourself comfortable on the sofa. Are you hungry?"

"A little," she admitted.

"I ordered a pizza for dinner. It should be here any minute. In the meanwhile, let me see what I can rustle up in the kitchen."

The only thing I managed to rustle up were some olives that had been sitting in my refrigerator for the past three years. Heidi had the good sense to turn them down. When I got back from the kitchen, I found Prozac curled up in Heidi's lap, doing her best to look adorable. Prozac loves to turn on the charm for guests. I get treated like a motel chambermaid, but for perfect strangers, she's Little Miss Affectionate.

"What am I going to do?" Heidi said, wide-eyed with fear. "The police think they've got another Menendez case on their hands."

"Are they sure it's murder?" I asked.

Heidi nodded solemnly.

"But why on earth would they think you did it?"

"I was the only one home. Daddy was at work. Brad was at school. And Conchi was away on her day off. And besides," she added miserably, "only about 90 million people at my birthday party heard me say I wished SueEllen was dead."

Oh, jeez. I'd forgotten all about that.

"Couldn't somebody else have gained access to the house?"

"I told the police about the blonde in the hallway, but I could tell they didn't believe me."

"What blonde in the hallway?"

"When I got home from school, I saw a blonde in a sweat suit going down the hallway to SueEllen's bathroom. She was walking away from me, so I couldn't see her face. I just assumed it was Larkspur. But it turns out Larkspur was working all day out in Santa Monica. So it couldn't have been her."

I wasn't so sure about that.

"The police think I'm making up the story about the blonde. I can tell by the way they look at me. Really, Jaine. I'm afraid they're going to arrest me."

"Heidi, honey," I said, trying to sound far more confident than I felt. "They're not going to arrest you."

"I didn't kill her. Honest, I didn't."

"Of course, you didn't," I said, taking her in my arms. If this kid was capable of murder, then I was capable of dieting. "Now how about a nice bowl of cereal?"

I'd long since given up on Sir Speedy, so I hustled Heidi into the kitchen, where I fixed us each a bowl of Cheerios. I was just glad I had milk in the refrigerator that hadn't turned solid.

Once we were settled back on the sofa, slurping down our Cheerios from chipped Flintstones cereal bowls, I said, "Tell me about the blondes in SueEllen's life."

"What do you mean?"

"Maybe the cops don't believe you saw a blonde in the hallway, but I do. Now let's try and figure out who it could be."

She shot me a grateful smile.

"Can you think of a blonde who might have had a key to the house? Or someone that SueEllen knew well enough to buzz in on her intercom?"

"Well, there's Larkspur, of course. But she was out in Santa Monica."

"So she says."

"And there's Ginny Pearson."

"Who's she?"

"SueEllen's best friend. They met years ago, handing out prizes on a game show. But she couldn't have done it. She and

SueEllen were very close."

"Any other blondes?"

She shook her head. "I can't think of any."

"What about your father? Any blondes in his life? Other than Larkspur?"

"There's Denise, the nurse at his office. I think she and Daddy are fooling around."

"What makes you say that?"

"Nothing, really. Just the way she looks at him. All gooey-eyed."

Wow. Between SueEllen, Larkspur and Denise, Hal Kingsley had been a mighty busy man. I was surprised he still had enough energy to perform tummy tucks.

"Does your father know you're here?" I asked.

She shook her head.

"I'd better call and let him know you're okay."

"Do you have to?"

"Yes, I have to. He's probably worried sick."

But Hal Kingsley didn't sound worried sick at all. He was his usual undemonstrative self when I told him that Heidi was sitting on my sofa. I had a sneaky suspicion that he didn't even know she'd been gone. I couldn't bear the thought of sending Heidi back to such a cold fish, so I asked if she could spend the night.

"I'll bring her back tomorrow," I promised.

Without a moment's hesitation, he said it was fine.

I hung up, wondering what it must be like having a father like Hal. My dad may have been running around with a used toupee on his head, but at least I knew he loved me enough not to toss me over to a virtual stranger in a time of crisis.

"Was Daddy worried?" Heidi asked.

"Very," I lied. "But he said you could sleep over."

Heidi sighed.

"Believe it or not," she said, "this is my first sleepover. I don't have many friends. Oh, who am I kidding? I don't have *any* friends."

"Well, you have one now," I said. "Me."

At which point, Prozac sat up and meowed.

"And Prozac, of course."

Damn cat hates to give up the limelight for a second.

"How about we get in our pajamas and watch a movie on TV?"

Minutes later, Heidi and I were curled up in bed, Prozac snuggled on Heidi's chest.

"You sure she's not bothering you?" I asked.

"No, no," she said, stroking Prozac lovingly. "She's a wonderful cat."

Prozac opened one eye and shot me a look that said, *Haha. Fooled another one.*

We zapped around and were lucky enough to find one of my all time favorite movies, *Roman Holiday*, with Audrey Hepburn and Gregory Peck. Heidi had never seen it and got caught up in it, which was a good thing. She needed all the distraction she could get.

It was near the end of the movie, when Audrey gives up Gregory (foolish girl!) and goes back to being a princess, when the doorbell rang.

I threw on my robe and went to the door.

"Who is it?" I called out. For an awful minute, I was afraid it might be the cops coming to arrest Heidi.

"Sir Speedy."

Oh, great. Only five hours late.

I opened the door, utterly disgusted. "It's after midnight," I said to the third world refugee who stood at my door.

"Sorry," he said in halting English. "My car busted down on freeway."

He handed me the pizza, which wasn't

136

even remotely warm.

"What are you, crazy? We're not going to eat this. Who eats cold pizza at one in the morning?"

Okay, so we ate it. Standing over the kitchen sink in our bare feet. Tossing the anchovies to Prozac.

"This is fun," Heidi said, slurping up a gooey strand of cheese.

At that moment, she reminded me of Audrey's *Roman Holiday* princess, running away from a life that gave her little pleasure, and enjoying herself for a change.

I was glad she was having fun. I only hoped it would last.

Chapter
Nine

I drove Heidi home the next morning, after a nutritious breakfast of pizza crusts and Pepsi. Conchi greeted us at the door, clutching her ever-present bottle of Windex. I was beginning to think she owned stock in the company.

"Miss Heidi!" she said. "Are you all right? I was worried about you."

I was glad to hear that somebody was.

"I'm fine, Conchi. Where's Dad?"

"Mr. Hal went to the gym to play racquetball."

He went to the gym? With his wife dead less than twenty-four hours and his daughter the prime suspect? What a prince. Meanwhile I could see Brad in the living room, sprawled out on a sofa, leafing through his Ferrari brochure, another grief-stricken mourner.

"I guess I'd better go unpack," Heidi said, looking none too happy to be back in the arms of her dysfunctional family.

"Remember, Heidi, I'm here if you need

me. And you mustn't worry about the police. I can't believe they really suspect you of anything."

I reached over and gave her a hug.

"Everything's going to be okay," I said. "I promise."

"I wish I could stay with you," she sighed.

"I do, too," I said. "But I'm sure your father wants you here with him." I wasn't sure of any such thing, but I knew he wasn't about to let his daughter move in with a struggling freelance writer on the wrong side of the Beverly Hills tracks.

Heidi managed a weak smile and headed upstairs.

"Keep an eye on her," I whispered to Conchi.

"Si, Miss Jaine," Conchi said. "I will try to protect her from the evil spirit."

"Evil spirit?"

She nodded solemnly, her eyes filled with fear. "The ghost of Miss SueEllen. She is here. In this house."

Oh, great. The one person in Casa Kingsley who seemed to care about Heidi was a few cards short of a full deck.

"If SueEllen's ghost is here," I said, "I know a great way to get rid of her. Just ask her to help with the housework."

Conchi looked at me, puzzled. "Sorry, Miss Jaine. No comprende."

"Forget it, Conchi. I was just kidding."

She smiled a nervous smile, as if she thought I was the loony one, and started spritzing Windex at a huge gilt mirror. A fat lot of good she'd be comforting Heidi; the woman was scared of her own shadow.

I said goodbye to Conchi and headed out the front door, just in time to see Larkspur pulling up the driveway in a lemon yellow Beetle.

"Hey, Jaine," she chirped, reaching in to the back seat of her car for her massage table.

Was it possible? Didn't she know that SueEllen was dead?

"You're here awfully early," she said, crunching up the gravel walk.

"Larkspur, haven't you heard the news?"

"What news?"

"SueEllen is dead."

"Holy shit."

She blinked her big blue baby doll eyes.

"She was murdered. Electrocuted in her bathtub."

"Oh, my gosh." Her baby blues grew even bigger. "I don't believe it. Do they know who did it?"

"Not yet."

"This is terrible," she said, absently raking fingers through her hair. "Is Hal — I mean, Mr. Kingsley — home?"

"Nope. He's playing racquetball."

"Oh," she said, standing there in a daze. "Well, then. I guess I'd better go."

She got back in her car and sat behind the wheel for a minute or so until she finally remembered to put the key in the ignition.

Larkspur seemed genuinely shocked. If she was faking it, she was a hell of a good actress. Of course, this was L.A., where everyone and their uncle is a would-be actor. So for all I knew, her shock was something she'd been rehearsing all morning.

Maybe Larkspur was faking it; maybe she wasn't. One thing was for sure: *I'd* been faking it when I assured Heidi that the cops didn't suspect her of murder. I'd have bet my bottom dollar she was their Number One Suspect. Which is why I decided to pay a little visit to the Beverly Hills cops.

A sand-colored building dotted with pretty pastel mosaic tiles, the Beverly Hills police precinct looked like something featured in *Better Homes & Gardens*. It was all so sparkle clean and upscale; I was sur-

141

prised it didn't have a gift shop.

I found the Clint Eastwood lookalike at his desk, barking orders into the phone.

"I want it right away," he was saying, his jaw rigid with determination. "And I don't want any mistakes."

He was probably ordering lab tests. Or fingerprints. Or maybe even an autopsy of SueEllen's body.

He motioned me to a seat in front of his desk.

"You sure you got it?" he snapped. "That's a Chinese chicken salad, dressing on the side. And a mocha frappuccino, hold the whipped cream."

So much for my autopsy theory; the guy was ordering lunch. Chinese chicken salad. Only in Beverly Hills do cops order Chinese chicken salad for lunch.

His lunch order complete, Lt. Webb hung up and turned his attention to me.

"Ms. Austen," he said, tapping the eraser end of a pencil into the cleft in his chin. "How can I help you?"

"Actually, I'm here on behalf of my client, Heidi Kingsley."

"Your client? I thought you were a writer."

"I am. But occasionally I work as a private investigator."

And it's true. I don't like to toot my own horn, but I've actually helped solve two murders. (Which you can read all about in *This Pen for Hire* and *Last Writes*, now available in paperback at a book store near you.)

"You have a P.I. license?" Webb asked.

"No, not exactly," I admitted. "But I really did help solve those murders. One in Hollywood last year, and one in Westwood."

Okay, so I do like to toot my own horn.

"Two whole murders, huh?"

I decided to ignore that.

"Heidi's afraid you think she killed SueEllen," I said.

Webb sat back in his chair, still tapping the cleft in his chin with his pencil. Maybe that's how it got so big, from constant pencil-tapping.

"Seeing as you've solved two whole murders," he said, with a most annoying smirk, "I'll tell you this much: We're not ready to charge Heidi with SueEllen's murder. Not yet, anyway."

Ouch. I didn't like the sound of that.

"What makes you think she could have possibly done it?"

"Two dozen people at her birthday party heard her say she wished SueEllen was dead. And the very next day, her wish came true. Plus, your client was the only one home on the day of the murder."

He grabbed a pad from his desk, and consulted his notes.

"Hal Kingsley was in his office. His nurse has vouched for him."

"Yeah, the same nurse who's having an affair with him. Not exactly the most reliable witness."

He looked up from his notes.

"Do you know for a fact they're having an affair?"

"No, but I'm pretty sure they are."

"We can't bring charges against a man because you're 'pretty sure' he's boffing his nurse. And besides, the receptionist also backs up his alibi. You think he's sleeping with her, too?"

"Quite possibly."

"Like I was saying," Webb continued, ignoring my valuable input, "your client was the only one home the day of the murder. Her father was in his office. Her brother was having lunch in the Beverly High football stadium with three of his buddies."

"Friends have been known to lie for each other."

"And the maid was away on her day off with her boyfriend."

I blinked in surprise.

"Conchi has a boyfriend?"

"A gardener. Works down the street from the Kingsleys."

Wow. Talk about inspirational. If a scared rabbit like Conchi could land a boyfriend, there was hope for all of us.

"What about the blonde Heidi saw in the hallway?" I asked.

"Oh, yes," he said, oozing skepticism. "The mysterious blonde."

"SueEllen's masseuse is blond. Maybe it was her."

"Afraid not. According to my records, Larkspur O'Leary was busy with clients."

"Couldn't she have sneaked over to the house between appointments?"

"Nope. She was out in Santa Monica all day. There was no way she could have driven to Beverly Hills and back between appointments."

"What about the neighbors? Did any of them see a blonde entering or leaving the house?"

"Nobody saw this mysterious blonde except Heidi."

Clearly, he thought Heidi's blonde was bogus.

"I hate to break it to you, Ms. Austen, but your client is the one person who had both motive and opportunity to kill SueEllen Kingsley. Now if you'll excuse me, I've got work to do."

I got up to leave.

"One more thing, Ms. Austen," he said, looking particularly Clint Eastwoodish. "I think I can manage this case on my own. This isn't Hollywood, or Westwood. This is Beverly Hills."

"Right," I muttered under my breath. "Chinese Chicken Salad Country."

I left Lt. Webb's office, more convinced than ever that Heidi needed my help. Webb clearly had Heidi pegged as a psychotic Cinderella who'd gone berserk and offed her evil stepmom. If he had his way, she'd soon be sharing His 'n Hers prison jumpsuits with the Menendez brothers.

I made my way past the suntanned Dudley Do-Rights and down to the parking lot where I retrieved my Corolla.

Of course, now that my gig with SueEllen had come screeching to a halt, I should have been home thinking up new slogans for my biggest client, Toiletmasters Plumbers. They'd been using their old slogan (*In a rush to flush? Call Toiletmasters!*) for several years, and they were ready to try something new.

For a few desultory moments I forced myself to think up slogans. (*At Toiletmasters, we take the plunge for you! Let us bowl you over with our prompt courteous service.* And others too flushworthy to mention.) But my heart wasn't in it. I couldn't stop thinking about Heidi. Webb didn't believe her story about the blonde in the hallway. If only someone else had seen the blonde, he'd have to take her seriously.

It wasn't until I was halfway home that I remembered SueEllen's Peeping Tom neighbor, the retired astronomy professor. The one with the all-seeing telescope.

Chapter
Ten

Professor Henry Zeller's magnificent Tudor house was set back from the street on a blanket of lushly landscaped grounds, within spying distance of Casa Kingsley. I parked out front, and headed up the front path, past an impressive array of rose bushes. When I rang bell, the chimes played the theme song from *The Sound of Music.*

Professor Zeller answered the door, an elderly man festooned with liver spots. I figured he was somewhere between eighty and a birthday announcement on the *Today* show. He wore khaki pants and a plaid shirt with a plastic pocket protector. Once a scientist, always a scientist, I guess.

"May I help you?" he asked, blinking into the bright sunlight.

I assumed my most official voice.

"I'm here investigating the SueEllen Kingsley murder."

"Oh, dear." He seemed flustered. "I already spoke with the police. Didn't see anything. Not a thing."

"I'm not with the police. I'm a private investigator. May I come in?"

He hesitated. "Can I see some identification first? Your license?"

What is it with people nowadays? They're such fussbudgets when it comes to inviting perfect strangers into their homes.

"Um . . . sure." I rummaged through my purse and whipped out some identification. I flashed it before his watery blue eyes, hoping he wouldn't realize it was my YWCA card.

No such luck.

"That's a YWCA card," he said, squinting at the print.

"Yes, of course," I said, pedaling furiously. "YWCA. Young Women's Criminology Association. We get kidded all the time about our name."

"The Young Women's Criminology Association?" He scratched his head, sending tiny flakes of dandruff fluttering to his plaid shoulders.

"So may I come in?"

He thought about this for a moment, then must have decided I wasn't a deranged maniac with a meat cleaver in my purse.

"All right," he said finally, ushering me in to the living room.

149

I took one look around and realized that *The Sound of Music* door chimes made perfect sense. The place hadn't been decorated since Julie Andrews was in dirndls. Lots of harvest gold furniture on an avocado shag rug. A grand piano covered with sepia-toned family photos. And over in the corner, an old console television that was probably still playing *The Ed Sullivan Show.*

"Won't you sit down?" he said.

I took a seat on a sofa that bore an uncanny resemblance to the one in Rob and Laura Petrie's house. More family photos were propped up on the coffee table in front of me.

"How can I help you?" he asked, lowering himself into an armchair.

"I'm representing Heidi Kingsley."

"Little Heidi?" He smiled fondly. "Such a sweet girl."

"Actually, the police think she killed SueEllen."

His watery blue eyes blinked in disbelief.

"That's impossible," he said vehemently. "She couldn't have."

Suddenly hope surged in my body. How could he be so sure Heidi hadn't done it, unless he'd seen the real murderer himself? Was it possible that he witnessed the

150

crime? Had he kept his mouth shut so he wouldn't have to confess he'd been using his telescope to look at naked ladies? Had I solved the case in less than an hour?

Now all I had to do was get him to tell me what he'd seen. I'd have to go slowly and gently.

"Heidi swears she saw a blonde woman going into SueEllen's bathroom at the time of the murder, but the cops don't believe her."

He squirmed in his chair.

"I was hoping you might have seen someone," I prodded.

"No, no," he said, wiping sweat from his freckled brow. "I saw nothing."

"Are you sure? SueEllen told me you're a retired astronomy professor. She says you own a telescope. Are you sure you just didn't happen to be looking through your telescope that day?"

"No," he insisted, "I saw nothing."

Obviously, the gentle treatment was getting me nowhere. I decided to go for the jugular.

"Look," I said. "I lied. I'm not a private eye. Not officially, anyway. I'm a writer. Last week I was working with SueEllen Kingsley, ghostwriting a book."

"So that was you!" he blurted out. "The

one on the toilet bowl. I thought you looked familiar."

Then, realizing he'd said way too much, he clamped his mouth shut.

"I saw you watching SueEllen through your telescope, Mr. Zeller. She told me you watched her all the time. So I'm asking you again. Are you sure you didn't see anyone that day?"

"No," he said, his voice shrill with fear. "I told the police, and I'm telling you. I didn't see anyone."

I knew he was lying through his dentures.

"I'm afraid you'll have to leave now," he said, hoisting himself up from his chair.

Then I spotted one of the photos on the coffee table. Of a teenage girl, with braces and bangs and freckles across her nose.

"This your granddaughter?" I asked, holding it up.

He nodded.

"What if the cops suspected her of murder? Would you sit by silently then?"

He looked at the picture, then at me. Then back at the picture.

"Okay," he said finally, crumpling back down into his chair. "I saw somebody."

"A blonde?"

He nodded. "She came into the bathroom while SueEllen was taking her bath."

"Did you get a good look at her?"

He shook his head. "No. Her back was to me; I couldn't see her face at all."

Damn.

"Then the phone rang, and I went to get it. It was one of those irritating telemarketers. By the time I came back, the blonde was gone, and SueEllen was dead."

He sat there, still stunned at the enormity of what he'd just missed seeing.

"You've got to tell the police," I said.

"I can't."

"Why not?"

"Don't you see? I'm in a most awkward position. If I tell the police what I saw, they'll know that I was watching SueEllen. It'll be in all the papers. They'll call me a Peeping Tom, a voyeur. My reputation will be ruined."

"I'm sure the cops will keep it out of the papers if you want them to."

"Do you really think so?"

"Of course."

"But what about my wife? When Emily finds out what I've been doing, it'll break her heart."

"Oh, Henry. Don't be a silly old poop."

I looked up and saw a pink butterball of a woman standing in the doorway, wearing gardening gloves and a big floppy hat. So that's who was responsible for those gorgeous roses out front.

Mr. Zeller's face turned ashen.

"How long have you been listening to us, Emily?"

"Long enough."

She whipped off her gardening gloves and strode briskly into the room.

"You think I don't know you've been peeking at that tart all these years?"

"You knew?"

"Of course," she said, pulling off her hat, and shaking out a halo of soft white curls. "What's the big deal? You watched SueEllen, and I rented Tom Cruise movies. Now get on the phone this instant and call the police. You've got to help poor Heidi."

The dear sweet woman. I felt like kissing the toe of her garden boots.

"Just tell them you were cleaning your telescope," she said, "and you happened to look in SueEllen's window."

Why hadn't I thought of that?

"All right, Emily." Professor Zeller kissed his wife on her powdery cheek.

"Oh, don't be an old mushbag," she said, shooing him away.

Then she turned to me.

"I made double fudge brownies for

tea. Care to join us?"

What did I tell you? The woman was a saint.

Two brownies later (okay, three brownies later), after thanking the Zellers profusely for calling the police, I bid them a fond farewell.

"You stop by any time you want, honey," Mrs. Zeller said. "I like to see a girl with a healthy appetite."

I drove back home, feeling quite proud of myself. True, Professor Zeller hadn't seen the actual murder. But he *had* seen a blonde. Which meant Lt. Webb would have to take Heidi's story seriously.

To atone for the three brownies I'd eaten (okay, four brownies), I made a solemn vow to skip dinner. I made this vow approximately half a block before pulling in to a Burger King and ordering a Whopper to go. I promised myself I'd eat just a few bites, then save the rest for breakfast. Which, incidentally, is one of the many things I like about being single. I can eat a Whopper for breakfast without The Blob lecturing me about healthy eating over his bowl of Froot Loops. Yes, I vowed, as I ordered extra fries, I'd just eat a few teensy bites and save the rest for breakfast.

I bet you think I came home and ate the whole thing in one sitting. No way. Unh-unh. As promised, I took a few bites and put the rest in the refrigerator. Where it sat for a whole thirty seconds before I got it out and snarfed it down, tossing chunks of burger to Prozac who stood yowling at my feet. Yes, I realize that a burger was the last thing I needed after four fudge brownies (okay, five fudge brownies), but I figured I'd just skip breakfast, thus not changing my planned calorie intake one itty bitty calorie.

After fighting Prozac for the last fry (Prozac won), I headed off to the shower. I still couldn't face the tub, not after what I'd seen yesterday.

Standing there under the hot spray, I realized how exhausted I was. Frankly, I hadn't slept well last night with Heidi in the bed. It had been ages since I'd shared a bed with another human being (if you consider The Blob human). I'd hovered on my side of the bed, trying not to move, afraid I'd roll over onto Heidi in the middle of the night. After an hour or so of this, I gave up and trudged to the living room, where I slept fitfully on the sofa.

Now I got out of the shower and toweled off, too tired to even consider blow-drying my unruly mop. I took a feeble pass at brushing my teeth, then slipped on my nightgown and headed to bed where I fully intended to spend the night spread-eagled, watching old *Lucy* re-runs.

For a minute, I just lay there, blowing my breath into my cupped hands and smelling the pickles and onions from my Whopper. I considered getting up and gargling, but decided to conserve my energy for something more important. Like reaching for the remote.

Minutes later, I was watching Lucy stuck in a meat locker, icicles dripping from her eyelashes, when the phone rang. I reached for it groggily, and Kandi's voice came booming on the line.

"So? Are you excited?"

"About what?" I yawned.

"Don't tell me you forgot!"

"Forgot what?"

"Oh, God," she groaned. "You did forget."

"What are you talking about?"

"Your date. With Ted Lawson."

I bolted up in bed.

Damn. Tommy the Termite. I'd forgotten all about him. What time did he say he'd pick me up? Seven-thirty. And it was now — aaack! — seven twenty-four.

"Kandi, honey, gotta run. He's gonna be here in six minutes, and I'm not dressed."

"Jaine, Jaine, Jaine," Kandi said, sighing deeply. "What am I going to do with you?"

"Okay, so I forgot. I've got other things on my mind."

Like a dead body floating in a bathtub, for one.

I hung up, after promising Kandi I'd meet her for brunch the next day to discuss the details of my date.

Then I tore out of bed and practically flew into my bra and panties. I threw on a pair of jeans and a black cashmere turtleneck, which I saw to my dismay was covered in cat hair.

"Prozac!" I shrieked. "How many times have I told you: No napping on my sweaters!"

Darn cat didn't even bother to look up from where she was licking her privates. Oh, well. There was no time to change. I'd have to stick with my cat/cashmere blend.

I pulled on my boots and hurried to the bathroom to throw on some blush. And then disaster struck: I saw myself in the mirror. Aaack! My hair! I hadn't blown it straight, and now I looked like Elsa Lancaster in *The Bride of Frankenstein*. At which point, the doorbell rang. I grabbed a rubber band and yanked my ball of frizz into a ponytail.

I only hoped Tommy the Termite didn't mind being seen in public with a woman with pickle-and-onion breath who looked like she'd just stuck her finger in an electric socket.

As I hurried to the door, I cursed myself for saying yes to this date in the first place. I wasn't ready for romance. Not now. Not yet. Not while the memory of The Blob still lingered in my brain.

And then I opened the door.

Standing there before me was a tall guy with dark curly hair and the kind of classically sculpted face you find on a Michelangelo statue or a daytime soap.

"You must be Jaine."

He smiled, revealing perfect white teeth.

"These are for you," he said, handing me a darling bouquet of daisies.

Hmmm. Maybe this dating thing wasn't so bad, after all.

Chapter Eleven

You know how it is when you're dreading something and you're dragging your heels and you finally force yourself to go, and it turns out to be a wonderful surprise and you're glad you made yourself do it?

Well, that may have happened to you, but it sure didn't happen to me. My date with Ted Lawson, aka Tommy the Termite, was an utter disaster, the Titanic of blind dates.

Sure, Ted was handsome. But he was also a self-centered, self-serving cheapskate egomaniac. And those were his good points.

At the beginning, of course, I didn't know all this. I was actually foolish enough to think it might be a pleasant evening. After putting the daisies in water and saying goodbye to Prozac, we headed outside to Ted's "previously owned" Mercedes. It was previously owned, all right. No doubt by a member of the Soprano family. I do not lie when I tell you there were bullet holes on the passenger side of the car. My first omen that the evening was not going to be the date of my dreams. An omen I should have paid attention to.

"I made reservations at a terrific restaurant in Westwood," Ted said. "You're going to love it."

So we drove over to Westwood Village, the Mercedes belching noxious plumes of smoke into the air. Ted spent the entire time talking about the traffic he encountered on the 405 freeway on his way to pick me up. (It was bumper to bumper all the way from Ventura to Santa Monica Boulevard, in case you're interested.) Okay, so it wasn't the snappiest conversation I'd ever heard. But I figured maybe he was nervous. Or maybe he was a traffic aficionado. I was willing to give him the benefit of the doubt.

About half a mile away from Westwood, he pulled into a residential street and parked the car.

"I thought we were going to Westwood," I said.

"We are."

"But it's at least a dozen blocks away."

"I know," he said, checking his profile in the rear view mirror, "I thought it would be fun to get some exercise."

Translation: *I'm too cheap to spring for valet parking. Or a parking lot. Or even metered parking.*

So we trekked sixteen blocks (but who's counting?) in the damp night air into Westwood. You'll be glad to know Ted had stopped talking about traffic on the 405. Now he was talking about traffic on the 110.

"You should have seen it. There was a semi jack-knifed across three lanes. Traffic was backed up for miles in both directions."

Well, at least those people were sitting comfortably in their cars, not clomping through the fog in tight boots. By now, my feet were killing me, and my hair was so wiry, you could've used it to scour pots.

At last we made it to Westwood.

"Right this way," Ted said, taking me by the hand. Up ahead I could see an Arby's. For a frightening instant I thought that's where we were going. After all, Ted had made me trek halfway across town to save a buck on a parking meter.

But no, he led me past Arby's to a charming restaurant nestled in an old brick building. Hmm. Maybe I'd misjudged the guy. Maybe he wasn't a cheapskate. Maybe he really did want to get some exercise. After all, he was an actor. He had to keep in shape.

The maitre d' greeted us warmly and led us to a cozy corner table for two. The place was tastefully elegant, with soft lighting, exposed brick walls, and a bud vase of fresh cut orchids at our table.

As I sat down, the waistband of my jeans dug painfully into my gut, thanks to those five brownies and the Whopper I'd snarfed down earlier. Why the heck hadn't I worn the elastic waist outfit I'd worn to Sue-Ellen's party? Oh, well. Maybe I could manage to sneak open the button on my waistband when Ted wasn't looking.

Our waiter (a slim young man whom I'll call Kevin because that's what nine out of ten waiters in Los Angeles are called) slipped us our menus.

"You don't mind if I order for both of us?" Ted asked.

"Yes, actually, I do mind. I don't like it when people presume to know what I feel like eating."

Of course, I didn't say that. I didn't have a chance to say that, because before I knew it, Ted was giving Kevin our order.

"We'll share a cup of soup, and two coffees for dessert."

Uh-oh. It was going to be an Arby's night, after all.

"Haha! Gotcha!" he said, poking me most annoyingly in my ribs, and then adding, "Somebody at this table could stand to work on her abs.

"Actually," he told Kevin, "we'll have the lobster bisque, heirloom tomato salad, chateaubriand for two, and crème brûlée for dessert. Make sure the soup is hot, really hot, and the steak is bloody rare. You like it rare, don't you, Jaine?"

No, I don't, but it didn't matter, because he didn't wait for me to answer.

"And bring us a bottle of the Jordan cabernet."

I happened to know that the Jordan cab cost sixty dollars. You know how I happened to know? Because Ted told me.

"This wine costs sixty bucks," he boomed, for all the world to hear.

It was a good thing I'd eaten that Whopper and five brownies. Because, as it turned out, Ted kept sending everything back. The soup was too cold, the salad was too warm, the wine was too "new," and the steaks were too well done.

I was convinced that the chefs and waiters were lined up in the kitchen taking turns spitting in our food.

By the time our corrected dishes were finally brought out to us, I had totally lost what little appetite I'd started out with.

Yes, it was truly the Dinner from Hell. I'd long since popped the button on my waistband. I didn't care whether or not Ted noticed. But he didn't notice. He was too busy talking about his favorite topic — Ted.

I heard about his childhood, his adolescence, his college years, his three ex-wives (all of them bitches), and his career. Oh, did I hear about his career. I heard about every part he'd ever played, starting with the time he played a rutabaga in his kindergarten production of *Our Vegetable Friends*.

I tried valiantly to tune him out, but I couldn't. His voice bored into my skull like a vise in a medieval torture chamber.

Not once did he ask me about myself. I stand corrected. Once. Here's how it went:

Him: "Kandi tells me you're a writer."

Me: "Yes, I —"

Him: "That's fascinating. I've always wanted to write a novel. And I've got a great idea, too. All about an actor in Hollywood. One of these days, when I've got a few weeks to spare, I'm going to write it."

And so it went, on and on and on, until I

wanted to impale him on my butter knife. Finally, our busboy cleared away our dinner plates. I'd barely touched my bloody rare steak. I couldn't. It was practically still alive.

"For a gal with your build, you're not much of an eater, are you?" Ted asked with all the subtlety of a Mack truck.

But I didn't care. He could hurl veiled insults at me all he wanted. Because at last I could see the light at the end of the tunnel. We'd finished the main course. Now all I had to do was make it through dessert and this ghastly ordeal would be over. Somehow I managed not to ball up my napkin and shove it down his throat while Ted rambled on about his life as a cartoon character.

Finally, I saw Kevin approaching with our dessert, a gorgeous crème brûlée. I was thoroughly disgusted with myself when I realized that I actually wanted to eat it. But the diet fairy must have been looking out for me, because just as I cracked open the golden crust with my fork, Ted whipped it away from me.

"Just a sec," he said, pulling a Baggie from the inside pocket of his sports jacket. And then, before my horrified eyes, he took out a dead cockroach and plopped it

166

into the crème brûlée.

"What are you doing?" I managed to gasp.

"Getting us a free meal. Don't worry," he winked. "This works every time."

He snapped his fingers, summoning our waiter.

Kevin, who'd grown to loathe us with each succeeding course, came warily to our side.

"Yes, sir?"

"What sort of a restaurant is this?" Ted exploded. "Look what we found in our crème brûlée. A cockroach. I want to see the manager."

By now the other diners were sneaking covert looks in our direction.

"No, no, that's okay," I said. "Accidents happen."

"Don't be silly," Ted said, shooting me a look. "I want to see the manager immediately."

Kevin scurried off to the kitchen. Minutes later, a red-faced man in a chef's toque approached our table.

"You're not satisfied with your meal, sir?" he said, smiling pleasantly.

"Of course not," Tommy boomed. Now the other diners were openly staring. "Look at this. A roach in our crème brûlée.

You don't expect us to pay for this meal, do you?"

"I certainly do."

Then he leaned over and said, not so pleasant any more: "We're on to you, asshole."

Ted blinked in surprise.

"This cockroach didn't come from our kitchen," the chef said, loud enough for everyone to hear. "It came from your jacket pocket. The busboy saw you take it out."

"That's a lie," Ted said, oozing righteous indignation. "You're going to take his word over mine?"

Then someone at a nearby table piped up. "I saw it, too. It was in a Baggie."

"Pay up," said the chef in a steely voice, "or I call the police."

And with that he plunked our bill down on the table.

Smiling feebly, Ted handed it to me. One hundred and ninety six dollars. Without the tip.

"Would you mind?" he said. "I forgot my credit card."

"You arrogant jerk! You expect me to pay $200 for the most hellish night of my life?"

Okay, so I didn't say that. No, my exact words were, "Do you take the Discover Card?"

By now, the whole restaurant was buzzing with excitement at this moment of dining drama.

Willing to do anything to end my misery, I forked over my credit card, and counted the milliseconds till Kevin came back with my receipt. I gave him a twenty percent tip for all the abuse he'd put up with. Then I asked him to call me a cab.

"Don't you want me to drive you home?" Ted asked. "Maybe we can stop off at Baskin-Robbins for a cone. I've got a two-for-one coupon."

I managed to fight back the impulse to strangle him.

"Go away, Ted."

"Can I call you some time?"

"No, you can never call me. Not under any circumstances. Not even if you should attain last-man-on-earth status."

"Your loss," he said, shrugging. "A girl with your thighs shouldn't be so fussy."

Then he got up and strolled out the door, but not before grabbing a fistful of mints on his way out.

I thought I'd wait inside until the cab showed up, but it was far too painful. People kept looking at me and shaking their heads, either in disgust or pity, I wasn't sure which. I could swear I overheard one of them say, "I saw her pop the button on her waistband."

No, I had to get out of there. I grabbed my purse and started for the entrance when suddenly I heard someone call my name.

"Jaine?"

Whoever it was, I prayed they were calling some other Jane, some Jane who spelled her name the sensible way.

"Jaine Austen, is that you?"

I turned around, and who should I see, but Mrs. Pechter. Oh, God. Now everyone at Shalom would know about my humiliation.

"Jaine, dear, come here," she said, motioning me to her table.

Smiling stiffly, I headed over to her table, where I saw that she was sitting with an absolutely adorable guy. Spiky sandy hair, green eyes, and an amazing smile. Really, this guy was cute with a capital C.

"Jaine, say hello to my grandson Morris."

This was Morris, the accountant? The grandson she wanted to fix me up with? I groaned softly. Did I really pass up a date with this dollburger to go out with Tommy the Termite?

Mrs. Pechter looked up at me through

her bifocals and shook her head, pityingly.

"Was that your boyfriend? The one with the cockroach?"

"He's not my boyfriend."

"So what were you doing having dinner with him?"

Would this nightmare never end?

"Oh, look, there's my cab!" I lied. "Gotta run. See you in class."

I hurried outside, where the fog had now turned to an ugly drizzle. The cab, of course, was nowhere in sight.

The valet parkers whispered among themselves; obviously they'd heard about L'Affaire Cockroach. I guess they must have felt sorry for me, because one of them asked me if I'd like some coffee while I waited for my cab. I nodded gratefully, and minutes later, he came out with a Styrofoam cup of coffee.

And as I stood there, huddled in the doorway, a well-heeled couple came walking by. The next thing I knew the man took out a ten-dollar bill and dropped it in my coffee cup.

Dear Lord. He thought I was a panhandler.

"Go get yourself a hot meal, honey," he said. "There's an Arby's down the street."

A perfect ending to a perfect night.

171

Chapter Twelve

I drove over to the Marina to meet Kandi for brunch the next morning, still fuming over my date with Tommy the Termite. Flashbacks from the evening kept playing in my brain like a trailer for a low-budget horror movie. I saw Ted chewing with his mouth full. I saw him snapping his fingers and calling the busboy "muchacho." I saw the cockroach lying belly up in the crème brûlée. And, most humiliating, I saw Mrs. Pechter's gorgeous grandson looking at me like I was something the cat burglar dragged in.

And to think, I had to pay two hundred dollars for all that fun.

Kandi was waiting for me on the patio of Tony P's, a casual dockside restaurant, where she'd managed to nab a table with a spectacular view of the Marina. Last night's fog had burned away and now the sun was shining on the million-dollar yachts, turning the scene into a picture postcard suitable for framing.

A storm cloud, however, was about to

erupt on the horizon. Namely, me.

I stomped over to the table where Kandi sat, perky and carefree, sipping a Bloody Mary.

"Hi, honey," she beamed, her eyes bright with excitement. "I ordered you a drink."

I plopped into a chair, and glugged down some of the Bloody Mary waiting for me on my placemat.

"So how'd it go last night?" she said, oblivious to my simmering rage. "I want to hear every detail."

"No, you don't," I said, through gritted teeth.

"It wasn't good?"

I laughed, a bitter laugh.

"I would've killed for merely 'not good.'"

"What happened?"

"Let's put it this way: Ted Lawson made The Blob look like George Clooney, Prince William and Denzel Washington rolled into one."

"You poor thing." She tsk-tsked sympathetically. "Tell Kandi all about it."

And I did. I filled her in on every excruciating moment, from soup to nuts. The "nuts" being Ted.

"Now it all makes sense," Kandi said when I was through. "I wondered why a handsome guy like Ted was so desperate for a blind date. I should've known there was something wrong with him."

Yes, I thought. *You should've.*

"And I can't believe you got stuck with the check."

"Two hundred dollars!" I reminded her. "Plus tip!"

"Well, it's all my fault. So I insist on picking up the tab for brunch."

"And I insist on letting you."

Kandi flagged down our waiter and ordered us huevos rancheros and two more Bloody Mary's.

"I don't suppose you want to hear about my date with Matt?" she asked.

"No, but you're going to tell me anyway, aren't you?"

"No, no. The last thing you want to hear is a fabulous date story," she said, dying to tell it.

"Oh, go ahead," I said, sucking the vodka from my celery swizzle stick. "I'm all ears."

So she launched into her latest True Romance tale — how Matt (aka Mr. Martial Arts) took her to a romantic Italian restaurant, where they drank chianti and ate spaghetti, and how they got up and danced in the aisle to a Dean Martin song, and how all the other customers applauded when they were through. I heard how they played kissy face in the parking lot, and how she was dying to sleep with him, but didn't want to seem like too much of a pushover, so she called it a night after after-dinner drinks at a cozy jazz club.

Thanks to my second Bloody Mary, I didn't mind listening to her. I was just happy not to be sitting across the table from Tommy the Termite.

She was somewhere in the middle of figuring out where she and Matt would live when they got married — his downtown loft or her Westwood condo — when she suddenly interrupted herself.

"Omigosh," she said. "In all the excitement of our dates, I forgot about that body you found in the bathtub. Whatever happened with that, anyway?"

Not wanting to take up too much time away from Mr. Martial Arts, I quickly told her that the cops suspected Heidi of killing her stepmom, and that I was trying to find the real killer.

"How do you know the kid didn't do it?" Kandi asked.

"I know. Just like I knew you weren't a murderer." (Yes, last year the cops suspected Kandi of murder, a ghastly episode in her life that you can read all about in *Last Writes*, now available in paperback, a fact I may have already mentioned once or twice.)

"Yes, but I'm your best friend," Kandi said. "Heidi is practically a stranger. Besides, this investigation stuff is dangerous. You could get hurt. Remember last year? You almost got killed."

That I did.

"Are you sure you want to be doing this?"

"Yep," I nodded, certain that nothing the fates threw my way could be as scary as what happened to me last night.

"Well, then. Just remember. In an attack situation, scream bloody murder. Kick 'em in the groin, and gouge out their eyes. And if they've got a gun, run. Matt says that a predator will hit a running target only 4 out of 100 times. And even then, it most likely won't be a vital organ."

"That's a comforting thought."

"I just want you to be careful."

"I'll be careful. I promise. Now, as long as you're treating, how about dessert?"

One lovely tiramisu later, we headed out to the parking lot.

The sun was shining, the gulls were swooping in graceful arcs in the deep blue sky, and the million-dollar yachts were bobbing merrily in the water. I was feeling a lot more mellow than when I first showed up. I could tell I'd mellowed out, because I no longer wanted to strangle Kandi. Maybe there was life after Tommy the Termite, after all. Maybe, in time, the memory of last night's debacle would fade. Never completely, of course. But enough to make me think of crème brûlée without puking.

As I stood there, pondering the nature of the human psyche and its ability to heal itself, who should I see driving in to the parking lot but Brad Kingsley? The lovely Amber sat at his side, running her fingers through his thick curls.

And you'll never guess what Brad was driving: A brand new cherry red Ferrari.

Brad tossed his key to the valet, and strode into the restaurant, Amber on his arm. King of the mountain. Top of the hill. If he saw me, he gave no indication of it.

"Wow," Kandi said, eyeing the Ferrari. "I'd kill for a car like that."

"You're not the only one," I said, wondering if Brad Kingsley had done just that.

Back in Beverly Hills, I lucked out and found a parking spot in front of my duplex.

As I headed up the front path, I glanced in Lance's living room window. Lance and a cute redheaded guy were sitting on the sofa, feet propped up on the coffee table, eating bagels. I was glad at least one of us was having a love life.

I let myself into my apartment where I found Prozac napping on the Sunday paper. She opened one green eye, and shot me a look that said: *What? No leftovers?*

"Sorry, Prozac. I was hungry. I finished everything. So sue me."

If she'd had the opposable thumbs to call a lawyer, she probably would have.

I made myself a cup of coffee and settled down on the sofa with the Sunday crossword puzzle. There's nothing I like better than whiling away a Sunday afternoon driving myself crazy thinking up a seven letter word for "African simian." You'll be proud to know I finished the whole thing in less than an hour, thanks to my razor sharp brain and three crossword puzzle dictionaries.

I was just reaching for the comics, when I saw the headline on the front page of the Metro section: *Police Search for Mysterious Blonde in Kingsley Murder.*

So Professor Zeller's call to the cops had paid off. Lieutenant Webb was finally getting off his ass and looking for Heidi's blonde.

And he wasn't the only one. I intended to look for her, too.

What's more, I intended to find her.

YOU'VE GOT MAIL!

To: Jausten
From: Shoptillyoudrop
Subject: IT'S BAAACK!

Horrible news. The toupee is back. We were sitting in the breakfast nook this morning, eating our cornflakes and bananas when the doorbell rang. It was the garbage man, with Daddy's toupee in his hand.

"I'm sorry, Ma'am," he said, "but we don't take dead animals."

Can you believe it? The ghastly thing keeps turning up like a bad penny. And now it's worse than ever. Before, it just smelled of Lysol. But now, after sitting in the garbage can with Taffy's cat food, it smells of Lysol AND tuna. Oh, honey. I'm simply at my wit's end.

To: Shoptillyoudrop
From: Jausten

Hang in there, Mom. Daddy can't possibly wear the wig, now that it's been fermenting in the garbage.

To: Jausten
From: DaddyO
Subject: Great news!

Great news, pumpkin. I got my toupee back. It's hard to believe that your mother would sink so low, but she actually threw it in the garbage. She admitted it. Said she'd do it all over again. But she won't get the opportunity. From now on, that toupee never leaves my head. She claims I can't possibly wear it, now that it's been sitting in the garbage. But she's wrong. I'll just wash it in Woolite and tumble dry low and it'll be good as new!

Your loving,
Daddy

PS. Here's a cute joke:
   What kind of coffee did they serve on the Titanic?
   Decaf!

To: DaddyO
From: Jausten

I seriously doubt your toupee is washable. Maybe you should make Mom happy and throw it away.

PS. Thanks for the joke, but I think the coffee on the Titanic is supposed to be Sanka. Because the ship sank. Get it?

To: Jausten
From: DaddyO
Subject: Are you sure?

Are you sure about that, honey? I don't think they made Sanka back then.

Chapter Thirteen

The next morning, after catching up on the latest in Daddy's toupee saga, I started hunting down blondes. First, I called Larkspur. Her machine picked up and told me to have "the best day ever" and to please leave a message. After promising to stop and smell the roses, I told her I needed to talk with her right away and to please get back to me as soon as possible.

Then I called Hal Kingsley's office, hot on the trail of Blonde Number Two, Hal's nurse Denise. Heidi said she thought Hal and Denise were having a thing together. I figured the only way I could observe the two of them in action was to make an appointment with the good doctor.

So I called and pretended I wanted the fat sucked out of my thighs. Of course, that was no lie. I did want the fat sucked out of my thighs; I just couldn't afford the thousands of bucks Hal Kingsley charged to do it. I'd be lucky if I could afford the consultation fee. Considering that I still hadn't been paid for the four days I worked for SueEllen, my bank balance was perilously low. Oh, well. I'd worry about that later. Right now, I needed to nose around Hal's office.

The receptionist informed me that the first available appointment was two weeks away. That would never do. I put on my most needy voice and told her how this was an emergency liposuction, that my high school reunion was coming up, and I couldn't face my former classmates with thighs the size of hamhocks. The receptionist, recognizing a true medical emergency when she heard one, managed to squeeze me in at 1:15 that afternoon.

My next blonde was Ginny Pearson, SueEllen's best friend from her game show days. Luckily, she was listed in the phone book and was home when I called. She agreed to see me that morning.

I assumed Ginny was another trophy wife, living in a mansion in Bel Air, busy with ladies' luncheons and bikini waxes and telling the cook what to make for dinner. So I was surprised to find her living in a modest apartment in West Hollywood.

The Hollywood Royale was a boxy stucco building with narrow balconies and ugly fiberglass curtains on the windows. I pressed the buzzer for G. *Pearson,* and she buzzed me into a tiny lobby littered with abandoned junk mail. I took the elevator up to the third floor and made my way down a corridor in desperate need of a paint job. Scuff marks from careless movers covered the walls. I suspected that tenants were constantly moving in and out of The Hollywood Royale. It didn't seem like a place you'd want to be stuck in for long.

I rang the bell to Ginny's apartment, and a willowy blonde in a black pantsuit opened the door. I could easily picture her pointing to an entertainment center on national television. There was something about her face that looked familiar. At first I thought I remembered her from one of her game shows, but then I recognized her. It was the blond waitress from SueEllen's party, one of the few friendly faces I'd seen, the one who gave me the baby lamb chops.

"Oh, hi." Her eyes lit up in recognition. "I remember you. Baby lamb chops, right?"

"That's me."

"Come on in," she said, ushering me into her living room, which looked surprisingly good, in spite of cottage cheese ceilings and cheap carpeting. Somewhere along the line, Ginny had picked up some good furniture. Big overstuffed pieces in pricey slipcovers.

I took a seat in one of the overstuffed chairs. Up close I could see the armrests were threadbare from years of use.

"So how can I help you?" Ginny asked, shaking her blond pageboy away from her face. "You said on the phone that you're investigating SueEllen's murder."

"Yes, I am."

"Did Hal hire you?"

"No, not exactly. I'm working on my own, on behalf of Heidi."

Her eyes widened with surprise. "Heidi?"

"Yes, the police think she might have had something to do with SueEllen's death."

"But that's impossible."

"Well, you heard what she said at the party. About wishing SueEllen was dead."

"Oh, come on. She's a teenager. They say things like that all the time."

"I know. It's ridiculous. But the cops are taking it seriously. And that's why I'm investigating. I thought you could help. Heidi tells me you and SueEllen were best friends."

"We were."

The way she said it made me wonder: Did she use the past tense because Sue-Ellen was dead, or because somewhere along the line they'd stopped being best friends?

"Forgive me for asking, but what were you doing waitressing at her party? Why weren't you a guest?"

She shrugged. In the bright morning sunlight I could see a web of fine lines around her eyes. "I needed the money. Even a place like this charges rent," she said, gesturing to the small apartment. "I waitressed at a lot of SueEllen's parties. SueEllen was kind enough to give me work."

Yeah, right. If SueEllen was so kind, why didn't she just write her a check, instead of putting her in the humiliating position of being her servant?

"So the two of you were really close."

"Well, not as close as we used to be, back in the old days. You know how it is. It was one of those friendships that you hold onto because of your shared history. I suppose if we met each other today, we wouldn't have been friendly. But back then, when we were first starting out, we were like sisters. We shared an apartment, not far from this one, as a matter of fact.

I'm afraid SueEllen got bitchier as she got older. I know she was pretty terrible to Heidi. But back when we lived together, she was a lot of fun."

She shook her head, lost in the memories of a kinder, gentler SueEllen.

"SueEllen was smarter than me, though. She always went for the rich guys. Me, I had a weakness for musicians. I didn't care about money back then. What a jerk, huh?"

"Do you know anyone who'd want to kill her?" I asked.

"Her caterer, maybe. She drove the poor guy nuts. But seriously, no. It's hard to believe anyone disliked her enough to kill her."

Hard for her to believe, not so hard for me.

"You know," she said, her voice cracking, "I still can't believe she's gone."

And with that, she wiped a tear from her cheek, the first tear I'd seen shed for SueEllen Kingsley since this whole mess began.

"I hate to ask you this," I said, feeling ashamed of myself for suspecting this lovely woman of murder. "But do you mind telling me where you were on the day SueEllen was killed?"

"Don't worry," she said. "I'm not insulted. The police asked me the same thing. I was working that day."

"Working? Where?"

"I'm a saleslady at Bloomingdale's. Hosiery."

"Oh."

How the mighty had fallen.

"You ever need an employee discount on pantyhose, I'm your girl."

Embarrassed by her display of emotion, Ginny reined in any further tears. She got up briskly, straightening the jacket of her pants suit.

"In fact," she said, "my shift starts in a half hour. If I don't hurry, I'm going to be late."

She got her handbag and keys, and we rode down in the elevator together, both of us trying to ignore the *Fuck You* etched into the faux wood paneling. I walked her to her car, a white Mercedes that had to be at least 20 years old. Another memento of the good old days.

"If you think of anything that might shed some light on the murder, give me a call," I said, handing her my card.

"Sure," she said. "Poor Heidi. She must be terrified."

Then she got in her car, and drove off to

the hosiery counter at Bloomingdale's.

As I watched the Mercedes disappear down the street, I wondered if Ginny secretly resented SueEllen's good fortune. Had she hated her for living in splendor while she was spending her days selling knee highs? Had she gone berserk with jealousy and tossed a hair dryer in SueEllen's tub? She said she was working the day SueEllen was killed. Could she possibly have slipped away on her coffee break, and bumped off her old roommate?

But Ginny seemed genuinely upset about SueEllen's death. That tear of hers looked convincing to me. It was possible she'd killed SueEllen, but not likely.

At least, I hoped not.

Dr. Frankenstein meets Laura Ashley.

That was the scene at Hal Kingsley's waiting room. Patients who'd just been taken apart and stitched together again sat around on dainty chairs, among pots of fresh flowers in flatteringly soft light.

When I showed up, there were two other patients there. One was a Chanel-clad dame whose skin had been pulled back tighter than a kettle drum. The other woman, in jeans and a leopard skin top, looked like she'd just gone ten rounds with

Oscar de la Hoya. A thick bandage strad-
dled her nose and, in spite of huge Jackie
O sunglasses, I could see a patchwork of
black and blue bruises ringing her eyes.

I thought about all the crazy things
people do in the name of beauty. At one
end of the spectrum, there were Dr. Hal's
patients and their fancy Beverly Hills face
lifts. At the other end was my father, with a
dead squirrel glued to his head.

I gave my name to a pert brunette at the
reception desk.

"Right," she nodded. "The emergency
liposuction."

She leaned over to get a look at my
thighs.

"Those are emergencies, all right."

Okay, so she didn't really say that, but
I'm sure that's what she was thinking. I
could tell from her size 2 waist that she
probably had thighs the size of broom-
sticks.

"Have a seat and fill this out," she said,
handing me a medical questionnaire. I sat
down in one of the dainty chairs, trying
not to stare at the prematurely embalmed
Chanel lady.

When I was through filling out my medical history, I checked out the magazines
neatly displayed on the coffee table. *Vogue*.

Elle. Harper's Bazaar. No *Good House-keeping* for this crowd. In the middle of the table there was a photo album, bound in sumptuous maroon leather. It was Dr. Hal's *Before & After* book.

I leafed through the photos, past wattle-free necks, chin implants, and chiseled noses. After a while I began to notice a similarity among the noses. All of them were straight and skinny with a little bump at the end. Wait a minute. That was Julia Roberts's nose. Good heavens. There was a whole army of women walking around Los Angeles with Julia Roberts' nose.

Just when I was thinking that Hal should be paying Julia royalties, I heard my name called out.

"Jaine Austen?"

The other two patients looked over at me, curious.

"No relation," I told them.

A buxom blond nurse stood in the doorway. I knew right away it was Denise. Mainly because she was wearing a name tag that said "Denise."

She had the hardened look of a truck stop waitress. Definitely a notch below SueEllen and Larkspur. Maybe Hal was tired of Ice Queens and New Agers. Maybe he was entering The Floozy Years.

"Right this way," she said, smiling stiffly. I wondered if her impressive set of boobs were part of her employee benefits package.

I followed her down a carpeted hallway. She wore her bushy blond hair pulled back in a pony tail. Heidi said the blonde in the hallway had straight hair like Larkspur. But as I knew so well from years of personal experience, even the curliest of hair can be tamed with a hair dryer.

She led me into a wood-paneled office, furnished with an imposing antique desk and leather club chairs. Hal was clearly going for the Lord of the Manor look.

There were two things that struck me about Hal's office. Number One, there were no photos of his wife and kids, the standard doctor's ploy to keep flirtatious female patients at bay. Perhaps Hal Kingsley didn't mind flirtatious patients.

The second thing I noticed was a door in the paneling behind Hal's desk. I wondered where it led.

"Have a seat," Denise said, "and the doctor will be right with you."

"I really appreciate your seeing me on such short notice. I know it must be a difficult time for the doctor."

For a minute, she looked as if she had no

idea what I was talking about.

"You know," I prompted. "What with his wife's tragic death."

"Oh, right," she said, finally remembering. Clearly SueEllen's death wasn't tops on her tragedy priority list.

"Yes," she said, as if reading from a prepared script, "we're all in a state of shock."

If she was in a state of shock, I was in the state of Hawaii.

"I guess Dr. Kingsley must be burying his sorrow in his work," I said.

"Right," she nodded, no doubt making a mental note to add *"burying his sorrow in his work"* to her script.

At which point, Hal Kingsley came striding into the room.

"Ms. Austen," he said. "Good to see you."

Then he glanced at Denise who lingered in the doorway.

"That'll be all, Denise."

"Yes, doctor," she said with a worshipful smile.

"So, Jaine," Hal said, consulting my file. "I see that you're interested in having liposuction on your thighs."

"That's right."

"Well, I must say, you're a perfect candidate for the procedure."

"Oh?"

"You know how this town is. I get women in here all the time with not enough fat on their thighs to butter a piece of bread. And still, they want liposuction. It's ridiculous. But someone like you, that's a whole other story."

Well, thanks heaps. What a thrill to learn my thighs were gargantuan enough to qualify for surgery.

"Of course, there are some risks, as there are with all surgeries —"

But before he could tell me what they were, his intercom buzzed. Denise came on the line with a mini-emergency. Apparently the beat-up looking dame in the waiting room had popped a stitch in her eye job.

"I'll be right back," he said, hurrying out of the office.

"Take your time," I said.

And I meant it. What a great opportunity to snoop. When I was sure he was gone, I made a beeline for the door in the paneling. I had to see where it led. I was just about to open it, when it suddenly occurred to me: What if it led to one of Hal's consultation rooms? What if I opened the door, and found a naked lady scratching her tummy tuck?

I took my chances and turned the knob.

No naked ladies, thank goodness. The

door led to an outside corridor, right across from a stairwell.

Very interesting. Hal said he was at his office the morning SueEllen was killed. But he could've sneaked out the back door and down the stairwell without being seen by anyone. Each of his patients would think he was tied up with another patient. Maybe Denise had been in on it with him. Maybe she lied to the cops, telling them he was in the office, when she knew darn well he was speeding across town to keep a date with a lethal hair dryer.

Of course, Hal couldn't have been the blonde that Heidi saw in the hallway. But maybe the blonde wasn't the killer. Maybe the blonde was an innocent visitor, and the killer was a dark-haired plastic surgeon.

Or maybe it was Denise who sneaked out Hal's back door and down the steps. I saw the way she looked at Hal. She was crazy about him. Perhaps even crazy enough to kill for him.

I shut the door behind me and turned my attention to Hal's antique desk. Did I dare peek in the drawers? After all, he could come back any minute. Oh, what the heck. I went for it. With my eyes constantly darting to the door, I started opening the drawers. Aside from a box of condoms in the bottom drawer, there wasn't much of interest.

And then I saw it, right there on his desk, for all the world to see (if all the world happened to be snooping in his office). A bill from his attorney. For a two-hour consultation, at a staggering $500 an hour. But that wasn't the part I was interested in. No, what held my attention was a yellow Post-it, in the upper right hand corner, with a handwritten note: *I told you when you married her — you should've made her sign a pre-nup.*

It looked like the good doctor had been consulting his attorney about a divorce. And he didn't have a pre-nuptial agreement. Which meant SueEllen could've taken him to the cleaners. A perfect motive for murder, don't you think?

Just then, I heard footsteps down the hall. I sprinted back to my seat, nanoseconds before Hal came striding back into the room.

"Sorry about that," he said.

"That's okay," I said, smiling graciously.

"So where were we?"

"You were going to tell me the risks involved in surgery."

"Oh, right."

"But before you do," I said, "maybe we

ought to discuss price. I'm not sure I can afford it."

"Ballpark figure," he said. "Including the anesthesiologist — eight thousand dollars."

"Wow, that's quite a ballpark."

"If you do your eyes at the same time, you save money."

"My eyes?"

"Just a tiny lift. It'll make you look refreshed."

"But I'm still in my thirties. Isn't that a little young for an eye lift?"

"Not at all. Plenty of my customers are in their thirties."

He took out a mirror from his desk and held it to my face. "See? The little lines at the corner?"

My God, he was right. I'd walked into his office with flabby thighs and now, out of nowhere, I had crow's feet, too.

"I can do both surgeries for $10,000."

Wow. What a bargain.

"I'm afraid it's just not in my budget."

"If your financial situation ever changes," he said, snapping my file shut, "I'll be happy to work with you."

I figured now was as good a time as any to bring up the matter of my unpaid wages.

"Speaking of my financial situation," I said, "I hate to bring this up so soon after

SueEllen's . . . um . . . passing, but I still haven't been paid."

"Oh, right," he said, a flicker of annoyance crossing his face. "How much was she paying you?"

"Three thousand dollars a week."

He shook his head and whistled softly.

"When I think of all the money she threw away on that book . . ."

He reached into his desk drawer and took out his checkbook.

"I didn't work the entire week," I said. "Just four days. That comes to twenty-four hundred dollars."

He dashed off a check, and ripped it out of the book. He'd obviously written a lot of these checks. SueEllen had been an expensive trophy wife.

"Here," he said, handing it to me.

I looked down at the check. He'd given me five thousand.

"That's for being so kind to Heidi."

"Thank you so much."

"Now maybe you can afford me," he smiled.

Was I imagining it, or was the good doctor flirting with me? Something told me those condoms of his were getting quite a workout.

"Oh, by the way," he said, as I headed

out the door. "We're having a memorial service for SueEllen at the house to-morrow. Three-ish. Please stop by if you can."

For the first time since he strode into his office, Hal Kingsley tried to look as if he actually missed his wife.

I thanked Hal for his time, and headed back to the reception desk to pay his outrageous $300 consultation fee. As I wrote out a check, I heard one of his patients say, "Dr. Kingsley says I have the face of a twenty-year-old."

Better give it back, I felt like telling her. *You're getting it wrinkled.*

After saying goodbye to the receptionist and my three hundred dollars, I walked out into the main corridor. But instead of going to the elevators, I took a detour and wandered over to the stairwell. I opened the door and poked my head in.

It was deserted, the way stairwells usually are. Personally, I find stairwells creepy; whenever I use one, I'm convinced there's a sex pervert lurking in a corner waiting to pounce. And I'm probably right. Hadn't Kandi said something about how people were seven times more likely to be attacked in a stairwell than in an elevator?

But for someone who wasn't scared of random perverts, it was an excellent way to leave the building without being spotted. True, Hal's office was on the sixteenth floor, and that was a lot of stairs, but Hal was in good shape. I could easily picture him — or Denise, for that matter — clomping down those steps on the day of the murder.

I wasn't about to try them myself, though; so I shut the door and headed over to the elevators. Just in time to see Denise getting on.

"Hold the elevator," I shouted.

She looked up and saw it was me, then hurriedly pressed a button. Something told me she was trying to avoid me, because immediately the door started to close. I stuck out my hand, risking elevator door amputation. But fortunately the door sprang back open, and I stepped inside. I was happy to see that Denise and I were alone in the elevator.

"Hey, Denise." I shot her a friendly smile, as if she hadn't just tried to ace me out of her elevator. "Sneaking off work early?"

"No, I'm not sneaking off work," she said, *tres* pissy. "I'm going down to the coffee shop."

"I was only kidding," I said. "I know you wouldn't sneak off work. You seem like a very devoted nurse."

"I am," she sniffed, somewhat mollified.

"That Dr. Kingsley," I said. "What a dreamboat. He must be so much fun to work with."

"Our relationship," she said, like a bad actress reciting her lines, "is strictly professional."

Yeah, right. If your profession happens to be call girl.

"I really was kidding before," I said, trying to ignore her icy vibes. "I didn't think for a minute you were sneaking off from work. Besides, if you were going to sneak away, you'd be crazy to take the elevator, not with the stairwell so close to your office. That would be the perfect way to leave the building without being spotted."

I watched her closely for a reaction. But she just stared straight ahead, expressionless. Damn. I was hoping she'd look nervous or worried, something that would confirm my stairwell theory. But her face was a mask. When the elevator door opened, she got out, without bothering to say goodbye.

It wasn't until the door slid shut that I

realized that she got off on the third floor. The coffee shop was in the lobby. Either she got off on the wrong floor by accident because I'd rattled her. Or she got off on the wrong floor on purpose to get away from me.

Either way, she was running scared. Which is something, I imagined, murderers often do.

Chapter
Fourteen

I headed home along Olympic Boulevard, wondering if Denise had bumped off SueEllen. I could just picture their final confrontation. ("My man-made boobs are perkier than your man-made boobs!")

Then suddenly I saw Beverly High coming up on my left. I remembered what Lt. Webb said about Brad having lunch on the football field the day of the murder.

On a whim, I turned left and pulled into the parking lot. The last time I'd seen this many luxury cars was the night of Heidi's party. Of course, not all of them were luxury cars. There were a few old clunkers there, too. Those were parked in the teachers' section.

I squeezed my Corolla in between a BMW and a Porsche with the vanity license plate HOT BOD. The campus intellectual, no doubt. Then I left the parking lot and wandered past various low slung buildings, until I finally came to the football stadium. At this time of day, it was deserted.

I took a seat in the bleachers and looked out over the empty field. How convenient, that Brad claimed to have eaten lunch here on the day of the murder. If he was the killer, it would be too dangerous to pretend he'd eaten at the school cafeteria. Even if his friends lied for him, he ran the risk that some nerdy kid would come forward and testify that he hadn't been there at all.

Of course, maybe Brad was telling the truth. Maybe he really did eat lunch out here in the football field.

Back when I was in high school, I never ate lunch in the cafeteria. A hotbed of snobbism, with a caste system straight out of Calcutta, the cafeteria was Hell with mashed potatoes — all the popular kids sitting together, all the nerds sitting together, and all the rest of us, floating somewhere in between, in awe of the caste above us and terrified of being contaminated by the caste below.

Which is why I joined the Art Squad. In a tiny cubicle in the basement of the building, my best friend Mara and I spent our lunch hours painting posters for the dances we never went to and the pep rallies we scorned. How safe we felt, tucked away with our egg salad sandwiches and acrylic paints, far from the frantic jockeying for social status in the cafeteria.

I was busy re-living the bad old days of high school, when suddenly the silence was shattered by shrill laughter. I looked up and saw The Enemy. A dozen or so cheerleaders were ambling out onto the football field for cheerleading practice. These were the girls I'd alternately loathed and envied in high school. The crème de la crème, the school beauties, every one of them sporting flat tummies and perfect hair.

But there was one girl who was prettier than the others. A knockout among knockouts. I recognized her right away. It was Brad's girlfriend Amber. She stood in the center of the line-up, her blond hair blowing in the wind, like a model in a shampoo commercial.

Out in the center of the field, the cheerleaders picked up their pom poms and broke out into their first cheer:

A ship, A ship, A ship A ship ahoy!
Beverly! Beverly! Oooooooh, Boy!

What a dumb cheer. It made about as much sense as an eye chart. But they belted it out with gusto, secure in the knowledge that girls as beautiful as they

205

were didn't have to make sense.

I felt like heading back to the parking lot, but I forced myself to stay. I wanted to talk to Amber. And so I sat around for the next forty-five minutes, watching the Beverly High cheerleaders shake their pom poms and flash their panties.

At last, they cheered their last cheer, and were heading off the football field, giggling and tossing their hair. I got up from the bleachers and started walking towards them. Suddenly it was high school all over again. I was The Untouchable approaching the Brahmins. Was it my imagination, or did I hear them suppressing giggles?

I told myself I was being silly. I was a grown woman and would not let myself be intimidated by a bunch of shallow teenagers. I sucked in my gut and walked up to Amber.

"Excuse me, Amber," I said. "Can I talk to you for a minute?"

This time there was no doubt about it. The girls looked at each other and smirked, the patented Popular Girl smirk.

"Do I know you?" she said.

"I'm Jaine Austen. I'm a writer. We met at Heidi's birthday party."

"I don't remember meeting you."

"Actually, we weren't introduced, but I was there."

"So? What do you want?"

Friendly little thing, wasn't she?

"Can I talk to you? Alone?"

"I'm sort of busy right now," she said, walking away.

"Maybe your boyfriend will be busy one of these days," I called after her. "At the state penitentiary."

That stopped her in her tracks.

"You guys go ahead," she said to her friends. "I'll catch up."

She headed back to me.

"What was that supposed to mean?" she asked.

"It means that Brad Kingsley is a suspect in the death of his stepmother."

"That's crazy. The police don't suspect Brad."

"I wouldn't be so sure about that."

"What have you got to do with all this? I thought you were a writer."

"I am, but occasionally I work with the cops as a private investigator."

Okay, so it was hogwash. But she fell for it.

"The police think Brad killed SueEllen?"

"They haven't ruled him out," I fibbed. "He said he was with his friends at the time of the murder. But we're not so sure that's true."

"He *was* with his friends," she said, defiantly. "I was there, too."

"You know, Amber, if you're lying to protect him, you're an accessory to murder. And in this case, an accessory is not a toe ring. It's something they put you in jail for."

If I thought that was going to intimidate her, I was sadly mistaken. Her green eyes narrowed into angry slits.

"Buzz off," she said. Only she didn't use the word buzz.

Then she turned and hurried after her friends.

"Nice talking to you, too," I called out after her.

Looked like I was back to being an Untouchable again.

"Tell me the truth. Do I have crow's feet?"

I hadn't forgotten what Hal Kingsley told me about the fine lines around my eyes. Now I sat across from Lance in my living room, sticking out my face for his inspection.

"They're worse when I smile, see?"

"Yes, you have wrinkles. But so does everybody. I'm telling you, nine-year-olds have wrinkles when they smile. Dr. Hal just wanted to make some extra bucks."

"Oh, Lance. You're an angel."

"That's what Jim tells me."

He grinned one of those goofy grins popular with people in love.

"So what's the latest on the SueEllen Kingsley murder?"

I filled him in on all the details, up to and including the convenient back door in Hal's office. When I was through, he filled me in on the details of his romance with Jim, up to and including a romantic candle lit dinner for two at the Four Seasons.

Let's recap here. Kandi gets a romantic Italian dinner and dancing in the aisles. Lance gets a romantic dinner at the Four Seasons. And I get a dead cockroach in my crème brûlée.

Life's just not fair, is it?

After Lance hurried off for yet another date with Jim, I called Lt. Webb. I was surprised to find him still at his desk. It was after six. I thought for sure he'd be out doing Pilates or eating sushi or whatever it is Beverly Hills cops do after work.

"Ms. Austen," he said. "What can I do for you?"

(Translation: *You again? What the heck do you want?*)

I told him about the Post-it from Hal's attorney, and how I thought Hal might have killed SueEllen to save himself an expensive divorce. And how the door in Hal's office led to the stairwell, and that either Hal or Denise could have used it to sneak out and kill SueEllen.

If you think he was grateful for my input, think again.

"I still think the kid did it," he insisted.

After we hung up, I poured myself a stiff chardonnay, hoping the good lieutenant would choke on a wonton in his Chinese chicken salad.

Then I called Heidi to make sure she was okay.

"How's it going, kiddo?"

"Honest answer?"

"Of course."

"It's great not having SueEllen around," she said, sounding more relaxed than I'd ever heard her. "You know what we had for dinner tonight? Kentucky Fried Chicken. Not some tiny ball of poached fish sitting on a piece of lettuce. And the funny thing is, without SueEllen on my case, I'm not eating nearly as much as I used to.

"Not that I'm glad she's dead," she added hurriedly. "I'm just glad she's not here."

"I understand," I said.

And I did. Sad but true. Sometimes a death in the family is just what the doctor ordered. And in this case, who knows? Maybe the doctor did order it.

"And now that the police are taking me seriously about that blonde in the hallway, I'm a lot less scared than I was."

Naturally I kept my mouth shut about my conversation with Lt. Webb.

"I owe it all to you, Jaine. If you hadn't gotten Professor Zeller to call the police, I'd still be their number one suspect. Really, I don't know what I would've done without you."

I hung up, and slugged down some more chardonnay. The poor kid had no idea how much trouble she was in.

Chapter
Fifteen

It was déjà vu all over again.

As I drove up the Kingsleys' circular driveway for SueEllen's memorial service, the same valet who'd taken my car at Heidi's birthday party came up to my window.

"You with the catering staff?"

How many times was I going to have to tell this idiot I wasn't a waitress?

"Nope," I snapped, tossing him my keys.

I headed inside where the same people from Heidi's party were milling around, now dressed in black.

Nothing had changed much since the night of Heidi's party: the people, the valets, the bar set up in the corner. The only difference was this time, everybody was happy.

Brad, whose brand new Ferrari I'd seen parked in the driveway, was out on the terrace, playing kissy face with Amber.

Hal was mingling genially among his guests. Every once in a while he'd remember to look solemn, but mostly he was smiling.

And SueEllen's lover, Eduardo. Last week when I saw him coming out of the Kingsleys' pool house, he couldn't have looked more miserable. Now he was leaning against the fireplace, making sexy small talk with a stunning redhead.

And of course, there was Heidi. What a difference from the night of her birthday party. Looking slimmer already in a simple black dress, she was sitting on one of the sofas having an animated discussion with Ginny Pearson.

I was glad to see Ginny out of her catering uniform and accorded guest status. Of all the people I'd seen so far, only Ginny wore the subdued expression of someone at a memorial service.

Heidi caught sight of me and came hurrying to my side.

"Hi," she said. "I'm so glad you came. Daddy ordered deli. The pastrami's really good."

She led me over to a buffet table heaped with cold cuts. Pastrami, turkey, ham, and cheese, with huge bowls of cole slaw and potato salad. A far cry from SueEllen's baby lamb chops and mushrooms en croute.

I helped myself to some pastrami and potato salad. Heidi was right. It was really good.

"Some wine, Miss Jaine?"

Conchi was at my side with a tray of drinks, skittish as ever, as if the ghost of SueEllen was about to show up and make her polish the silver.

"Thank you, Conchi," I said, taking a glass.

Then she scurried off to serve the other guests.

"How was the funeral service?" I asked Heidi.

Heidi shrugged. "The minister kept calling her SueAnn by mistake. Brad and Amber were practically necking in the back pew. And the only person who cried was Ginny."

"Didn't anybody from SueEllen's family show up?"

"No. Nobody."

That was odd. I wondered what happened to that rich old aunt of hers. Aunt Melanie. Probably dead and buried long ago. But what about her parents? Where were they? Had SueEllen alienated everyone in her old family, just as she'd done in her new one?

"Heidi, honey, don't you look nice!"

One of SueEllen's social string beans was at our side.

"Come say hello to my nephew. I've been wanting to introduce you two for ages."

She dragged Heidi over to a chubby kid in horn rimmed glasses. I felt like telling her that this was a memorial service, not a prom.

My glass of chardonnay in hand, I wandered around, watching the guests laugh and chat gaily, as if SueEllen hadn't just been lowered into the ground a few hours ago. When I go, I hope somebody remembers me at my own funeral.

I wandered around some more, past lively groups of people scarfing down cold cuts. And then, without quite realizing what I was doing, I found myself drifting up the stairs and heading towards SueEllen's bathroom. I don't know why I did it; I guess I hoped I'd find something there, something the cops overlooked, some clue that would lead me to her killer.

Just as I reached the bathroom, I felt a frisson of fear. Suddenly, returning to the scene of the crime didn't seem like such a hot idea. I told myself to stop being ridiculous. Nothing was going to happen. I was as bad as Conchi. I took a deep breath, and forced myself to open the door.

The room was dark, lit only by a few votive candles.

And that's when I saw SueEllen, lying naked in the empty tub. Oh, God. Either she was back from the dead, or somebody had put hallucinogens in the pastrami!

"Hey, babe," she said. "What took you so long?"

Wait a minute. That wasn't SueEllen's voice. It was someone a lot younger. If I wasn't mistaken, it was the voice of Beverly High's head cheerleader. I peered through the darkness, and sure enough, I saw that it was Amber stretched out in the tub like a Playboy centerfold, her eyes shut in ecstasy.

"Come here, babe," she cooed. "I can't wait to get my hands on you."

"Really?" I said, flipping on the light. "I didn't think I was your type."

Her eyes shot open.

"Jesus! What the hell are you doing here?"

"I came to take a tinkle," I lied. "How about you? Playing *Let's Boink in Dead Stepmommie's Bathtub?*"

Then I turned and made a dignified exit, just missing the loofa sponge Amber threw at me.

★ ★ ★

Back downstairs, I hurried to the bar for a refill on my chardonnay. After a few calming gulps, I looked around and saw that Nurse Denise had shown up. She was standing awkwardly in a corner, clutching a cocktail. With her bushy hair and too-tight dress, she was way out of place among the sleek Beverly Hills fashionistas.

I followed her gaze to where Hal was standing, talking to Larkspur. Larkspur looked particularly lovely that day, her blond hair cascading onto the shoulders of her slim black suit. She and Hal were chatting casually, but you could tell by the way they were looking at each other that there was something going on between them. I saw it. And so did Denise, who glugged down her drink with alarming speed.

Poor Denise. If she'd killed SueEllen hoping to be the next Mrs. Hal Kingsley, she was in for a big disappointment.

"Those two aren't wasting any time, are they?"

I turned to see Eduardo at my side.

"I don't believe we've met," he said, flashing me a devastating smile. "I'm Eduardo Jensen."

He held out his hand and I shook it. In spite of myself, I felt my knees go weak.

This was one stunning guy. That slicked back hair, those incredible cheekbones, and those amazing blue eyes that looked even bluer against his deep tan. Let me tell you, my G spot was jumping. But one of my major principles in life is to never fall for guys whose waistlines are smaller than mine, so I reined in my lust. Just barely.

"I'm Jaine Austen," I managed to say.

"Love your books."

I smiled weakly. If I had a dime for every time I've heard that line, I'd be independently wealthy and living in the south of France.

"So, how do you know the deceased?" he asked.

"I was helping SueEllen write a book."

"Ah, yes. The book. *Entertaining for Dummies*, or whatever she was calling it. She could have called it *Famous Recipes I Have Stolen*."

Another devastating smile.

"And you?" I asked. "How did you know SueEllen?"

I wanted to hear how he'd answer that one.

"I'm a friend of the family," he said, smooth as silk. "Both Hal and SueEllen have been kind enough to buy some of my paintings."

"Oh. So you're an artist."

"I try to be," he said, shrugging his shoulders with false modesty.

"I'd love to see your work," I said.

Not really. But I figured it was a good way to talk to him without raising his suspicions. I remembered how SueEllen had threatened Eduardo the night of Heidi's party. How she swore she'd tell everyone his dirty secret. But SueEllen had been killed before she had a chance to open her mouth. Was Eduardo the one who'd silenced her? I intended to find out.

"Maybe I could stop by your studio," I suggested.

"I'd like nothing better," he said, oozing sexual innuendo.

He gave me his card, and I made a date to drop by his studio the following day.

He took my hand, and kissed it. "Always a pleasure to meet an art lover."

And then he headed off to turn somebody else's knees to jello.

It took me a minute or two to recover from Hurricane Eduardo but when I did I saw that Hal had left Larkspur and was now talking to Denise, who looked none too happy. She gestured angrily at the lovely Larkspur, who was heading toward the door.

I left the two of them to duke it out, and quickly intercepted Larkspur before she could leave.

"Hey, Larkspur."

"Oh, hello, Jaine. Sorry I didn't return your call; I've been really busy. Heidi tells me you're investigating SueEllen's murder."

"As a matter of fact, I am."

"I don't know anything whatsoever that could help you," she said, her lips sealed tighter than a Hal Kingsley facelift.

No way was I going to get any information from her. Not unless I was sneaky.

"Actually, I wasn't calling about the murder."

"You weren't?"

"No, I wanted to set up an appointment for a massage. SueEllen told me how terrific you are."

Her face relaxed into a smile.

"Oh, how nice."

Then a tiny worry line marred her perfect brow.

"I'm pretty expensive," she warned.

"That's okay," I said. How bad could it be?

"Two hundred an hour."

Yikes. It's a good thing I had Hal's check in my purse.

"No problem," I said. "I don't suppose you have any available slots tomorrow."

"As a matter of fact, what with Sue-Ellen's passing, I do have some free time tomorrow."

I gave her my address and she said she'd be there the next afternoon at three.

Then I headed back to the buffet table for an eeny weeny snack. Maybe a pickle, or some cole slaw. I was determined not to eat one more bite of that fattening pastrami. And you'll be pleased to learn I didn't.

I ate the fattening corned beef instead.

I was standing at the buffet table, loading it onto my plate, when Heidi showed up at my side.

"Can you believe that woman?" she said, eyeing the social string bean who'd dragged her away from me. "Just because her nephew and I are both chubby, she thought we'd like each other."

"And did you?"

She blushed.

"He was okay, I guess."

Welcome to the wonderful world of teenage hormones.

"Oh, look," she said, eager to change the subject. "There's Grandma!" She waved to a stocky gray haired woman, coming down the stairs. "She just flew in from back East."

Heidi's grandmother clomped over to us in sensible support shoes. Her spiky salt and pepper hair hadn't seen a stylist in years. Like Nurse Denise, she was definitely out of place in this crowd.

"Grandma, I'd like you to meet my friend Jaine Austen."

"Nice to meet you, hon."

Right away I gave her points for not saying "Love your books."

"You must be Heidi's maternal grandmother," I said, working on the assumption that this stocky peasant woman couldn't possibly have given birth to the aristocratic Hal Kingsley.

"No," she said. "I'm Hal's mother."

"Really?" I said, blinking in surprise. "Well, nice to meet you, Mrs. Kingsley."

"It's not Kingsley," she snorted. "It's Kosciusko. Hal changed it when he moved out here and became a big shot plastic surgeon."

Why was I not surprised? This was Los Angeles, where everybody writes — and rewrites — their own life scripts.

"Heidi told me what a good friend you've been." She put her arm around her granddaughter and gave her an affectionate squeeze. "She could use a good friend. Frankly, I hate to speak ill of the dead, but that SueEllen was a stinker."

She wasn't going to get any argument from me.

"I knew she was trouble the minute she came on the scene. Now *that's* the girl Hal should have married."

I followed her gaze to one of the sofas, where Ginny was chatting with Hal.

"Yes, if only he'd married Ginny like he was supposed to, this poor child would've been a lot better off."

Hello. This was news to me.

"Hal was supposed to marry Ginny?"

"Oh, yes. He gave her a ring and set the date. Everything was fine until SueEllen decided she wanted him."

Okay, folks. Let's rewind the tape. What was all that malarky Ginny told me about only dating musicians? She never mentioned having a fling with Hal. If SueEllen had stolen Hal away from her, then Ginny might've hated her all these years. I could easily picture Ginny in her crappy apartment, thinking about SueEllen living in splendor, and saying to herself, *That should've been me!* Yes, Ginny could've been harboring a giant resentment, all right. One that might have exploded in murder.

Rats. The one person I thought couldn't possibly have done it was back in the running.

Chapter
Sixteen

I drove home on Suspect Overload, my mind reeling with murder scenarios. It seemed like anybody could have killed SueEllen. Hal, Brad, Eduardo, Larkspur, Nurse Denise, or — much to my dismay — the likeable Ginny. Who knows? Maybe Grandma Kosciusko flew in a few days early and bumped off her annoying daughter-in-law.

It was time to take out my trusty legal pad and write out a list of suspects. Writing things out, I've discovered, helps me clarify my thoughts. And at this point, my thoughts needed all the clarifying they could get.

"Hi, honey. I'm home," I called out as I let myself into my apartment.

Prozac looked up from where she was napping on my pantyhose and yawned.

"Just once," I said, sweeping her up in my arms, "can't you be excited to see me?"

As if in answer to my request, she started licking my face, like a puppy in a Hallmark commercial.

"Prozac, honey, I didn't know you cared."

And then, of course, I realized why she was playing kissy face. It was the deli. She smelled pastrami and corned beef on my breath. She leapt out of my arms and started running around my ankles in crazed circles, which is cat talk for *When do we eat?*

"Prozac, sweetie, I didn't bring home any leftovers."

She continued her ankle dance.

"Seriously," I said. "No pastrami. No corned beef."

I headed to the kitchen, Prozac at my heels, meowing loudly. *I prefer my pastrami as lean as possible,* is what I think she was trying to tell me.

I took out a can of cat food from the cupboard.

"Look, Prozac, your favorite. Fancy salmon guts."

Suddenly the dancing stopped. She shot me an injured look.

"Prozac, I'm sorry. There were no doggie bags. What did you expect me to do? Stuff my purse with cold cuts?"

I don't see why not, she meowed.

I opened the salmon guts and put it in her bowl. She sniffed at it, and walked away.

"Okay, don't eat it," I called after her. "Starving cats in Asia would be thrilled to eat fancy salmon guts! Starving cats in Asia would be happy to *have* dinner, and not *be* dinner!"

I let her sulk on the sofa; sooner or later she'd get around to eating. In the meanwhile, I had work to do. I sat down at my dining table with a legal pad, and started writing.

My Suspects
By Jaine Austen

Hal Kingsley: Unfaithful husband. Indifferent father. Was he tired of paying the upkeep on a trophy wife? Did he bump off SueEllen to save himself the trauma and expense of a messy divorce? He could have easily slipped away from his office and done the dirty deed. Or did he get someone else to do it for him? Someone like . . .

Nurse Denise: Could've been the blonde Heidi saw in the hallway. Did she kill SueEllen, hoping Hal would marry her once he was a free man? She was obviously crazy about the guy. But was she crazy enough to kill for him?

Larkspur O'Leary: Hal's New Age nymphette. Maybe she bumped off SueEllen to clear the decks for matrimony. But the cops say she was with clients all morning. Was she, really? Could she have somehow slipped away? Was she as ditsy as she seemed? Or was she a smart cookie just waiting to trade in the name Larkspur O'Leary for Mrs. Hal Kingsley?

Ginny Pearson: In spite of her generosity doling out baby lamb chops, could she possibly be a killer? Had she been seething with resentment because SueEllen had stolen her man and robbed her of a life of luxury? Did she sneak off from her job selling Bloomie's pantyhose and fry SueEllen with a hair dryer?

Eduardo Jensen: SueEllen's lover. Maybe SueEllen gave him a key to the house, so he could let himself in for secret sexfests. Maybe he used that key on the day of the murder and killed SueEllen to keep her from telling the world his dirty secret. Note to self: Find out dirty secret.

Heidi Kingsley: Had the motive. Had

the opportunity. Still can't believe she did it.

Unlike her brother . . .

Brad Kingsley: Says he was with his friends at the time of SueEllen's death. But the friends could be lying. Easy to picture a skunk like Brad sneaking home from school and killing SueEllen for a new HAIRBALL —

No, I didn't think Brad had killed SueEllen for a hairball. I was going to write the word "Ferrari," but that's when Prozac, still miffed over the pastrami affair, decided to sit on my list and cough up a hairball.

I was just about to give her a stern lecture when I looked at the kitchen clock and saw that it was six-thirty. My memoir writing class at the Shalom Retirement Home started in a half hour. I grabbed my car keys and ran.

If there was one thing I didn't feel like doing that night, it was teaching my class. What if Mrs. Pechter told my students about my humiliating date at the restaurant? What if they thought I was the kind of person who dropped cockroaches into crème brûlées to get a free meal?

Reluctantly I strapped myself into the Corolla and headed over to Shalom, hoping to catch all the red lights. Anything to delay the inevitable. But wouldn't you know, for one of the few times in my life as a Los Angeles driver, I positively whizzed along. Never have I seen so many green lights. Traffic was so snarl-free, I could've sworn I was in Omaha.

Before I knew it, I was pulling into the parking lot at Shalom. Oh, well. There was no getting out of it. I gathered my courage and my Altoids (I'm afraid I still had pastrami on my breath), and headed inside to face my students.

As it turned out, the last thing on my students' minds was my social life. All they wanted to talk about was SueEllen's murder.

"Jaine, honey," Mrs. Pechter said. "We saw in the paper that you found the body."

"That must've been horrible," Mrs. Rubin said, clucking sympathetically.

"What did she look like?" Mr. Goldman asked. "Were her eyes all buggy? Was her body blue? Did she have big bazooms?"

"Oh, Abe. Stuff a sock in it."

"Hey, inquiring minds want to know."

"Actually, class," I said, "I think we should get to our essays —"

"Yes, let's leave poor Jaine alone," Mrs. Zahler piped up.

"Poor Jaine?" Mr. Goldman sniffed. "If you ask me, we're the ones who should be scared. Every time she shows up, somebody drops dead. Remember that actor she worked with on the TV show? He dropped dead. Then she works for this socialite dame, and she drops dead, too."

Then he turned to me.

"With your track record, cookie, did you ever think maybe it's not such a hot idea to be working at an old folks home?"

Mrs. Pechter gave an aggravated humph.

"Just take your blood pressure medication, Abe, and you'll be safe."

"So," I said, determined to get the class back on track, "who wants to read their essay?"

Mrs. Zahler's hand shot up. Thank heavens.

"Mrs. Zahler?"

"It says in the paper that Mrs. Kingsley's husband is a plastic surgeon. You think she had a nose job?"

"I really don't know."

"Of course it was a nose job," Mr. Goldman shouted.

"How do you know, Mr. Smartie?" Mrs. Pechter challenged.

"Yeah," echoed Mrs. Rubin. "How do you know?"

"I saw her picture. I know a nose job when I see one." And then he threw out an intriguing challenge to the rest of the class. "You name a person, and I'll tell you if they've had a nose job."

"Sounds like a fun game, Mr. Goldman," I said. "Maybe you should play it after class. Right now, we're going to read essays."

I was quite pleased with my authoritative tone.

"Steve McQueen," Mr. Goldman said, ignoring me. "He had a nose job."

"Don't be ridiculous, Abe," Mrs. Zahler groaned.

"And Elizabeth Taylor."

"That's absurd," said Mrs. Pechter. "She's had the same nose since she was a little girl in *National Velvet*."

Mr. Goldman glared at her over his bifocals. "Elizabeth Taylor. Sissy Spacek. And Ernie Borgnine."

"That's crazy. Ernest Borgnine has a big nose."

"You should've seen it before his nose job." Mr. Goldman nodded smugly.

"Okay, class," I said firmly. "No more nose jobs. I want to hear an essay. Who's got one for me?"

They could tell I meant business. Either that, or they were sick of listening to Mr. Goldman. Mrs. Rubin raised her hand.

"Okay, Mrs. Rubin. Let's hear it."

She cleared her throat and started reading.

"*My Trip to Great Britain, England.*"

And so began the story of Mrs. Rubin's trip to "Great Britain, England." It was a stirring saga, the highlights of which included a Tour of Big Ben, the changing of the guards at Buckingham Palace (where Mrs. Rubin swore she saw Queen Elizabeth waving from the palace window) and finally, a trip to a genuine British pub for shepherd's pie and fish and chips, followed by a trip to a genuine British drug store for emergency supplies of Kaopectate.

So what if it wasn't Frank McCourt? At least, we were back to reading essays.

"Any comments?" I asked when Mrs. Rubin was through.

Mr. Goldman's hand shot up.

"Yes, Mr. Goldman?"

"Queen Elizabeth," he said, nodding cryptically.

"What about her?"

"She had a nose job."

Somehow I managed to restrain myself from choking him.

After slogging through a few more essays, it was finally time to call it a night. My students got up from their seats and started gathering their purses and back support cushions.

"Mrs. Pechter," I called out, "would you mind staying after class a minute?"

The others exchanged curious glances and reluctantly filed out of the room as Mrs. Pechter waddled over to me.

"Yes, darling? What is it?"

I'd simply tell her that Tommy the Termite was not my boyfriend, and that I was open and available for dating her adorable grandson.

"Actually," I said, "I wanted to explain about the man you saw me with the other night in the restaurant."

"Oh. Your boyfriend."

"No, that's what I want to tell you —"

"Listen, honey. You don't owe me any explanations. To each his own, that's what I always say. You want to go out with a guy who keeps a cockroach in his coat pocket, that's your decision. I'm just glad I'm not your mother."

"You don't understand. That awful man isn't my boyfriend. It was a blind date. A one-time mistake of horrendous proportions."

"A blind date? But when I asked if you'd like to meet my grandson Morris, you said you had a boyfriend."

"I know. I'm sorry. I lied, because at the time I thought I wasn't ready to date."

Mrs. Pechter blinked, puzzled.

"If you weren't ready to date, why did you go out on a blind date?"

This wasn't going to be quite as easy as I'd thought.

"My girlfriend pressured me into it. I didn't want to. Honest."

"Well, I certainly can see why you're not ready to date, if that's the kind of dates you go out on."

"Actually, Mrs. Pechter, I've been giving it a lot of thought, and I've decided that maybe I am ready to date. In fact, I would've never turned down a date with your grandson if I'd realized what a stud-muffin he was."

Okay, so I didn't really say that. What I said was: "In fact, your grandson seemed so nice, maybe I could give dating another try."

"No, no," she said, shaking her head. "If you're not ready to date, you're not ready."

"But I am ready. Really."

"No, darling. Rose Pechter is not a pushy person. I know how things are. I watch Dr. Phil. You need your space."

"I've got plenty of space. I'm not feeling the least bit hemmed in emotionally. It might be the perfect time to start dating."

"You're just saying that to be nice. You're afraid I'm hurt because you turned down my Morris."

"I'm not just saying it to be nice. I swear. I'd be happy to go out with your Morris."

"He's not a big time actor with insects in his coat pocket."

"That's okay," I said. "Here's my number." I thrust my business card into her hand. "Just give it to him. Please?"

By now I was practically on my knees.

"Okay, darling," she shrugged. "Whatever you say." Then she dropped my business card in her cavernous purse, and waddled out of the room.

I wiped the sweat from my brow, exhausted from all that grovelling. That had to have been one of the more humiliating experiences of my life. But, on the plus side, the adorable Morris might give me a call. I sincerely doubted it, but who knew? And even more important, at least Mrs. Pechter hadn't told the class about my disastrous date with Tommy the Termite.

Or so I thought.

Because just then, Mr. Goldman popped his head in the door.

"Hey, cookie," he said with a wink. "Ate any good cockroaches lately?"

YOU'VE GOT MAIL!

To: Jausten
From: Shoptillyoudrop
Subject: Worse than ever

Well, your father washed his toupee, and it's worse than ever. All the little clumps of hair are matted together, like a squirrel on a bad hair day. And it still smells like tuna.

This afternoon, I let Daddy talk me into going to the movies. As much as I hate to be seen in public with him, I really needed to get out of the house. Anyhow, there we were, watching the coming attractions, when someone behind us said, "Yuck. I smell rancid fish."

I was so humiliated, I couldn't even enjoy the movie. I felt just like Earlene's first husband Lester must have felt before he went to buy those Milk Duds and never came back.

Honey, you've got to write to Daddy, and get him to stop wearing that toupee.

Your desperate,
Mom

To: Shoptillyoudrop
From: Jausten

I've already tried, Mom. But you know how stubborn Daddy is. He won't listen to me.

To: Jausten
From: Shoptillyoudrop

Well, I just don't know what I'm going to do. I certainly can't go on living with a man who wears a dead squirrel on his head. If he won't give it up, I'll have no choice but to move in with you for a while, honey.

To: DaddyO
From: Jausten
Subject: If You Care Anything about Mom's Feelings

Daddy, if you care anything about Mom's feelings, you'll stop wearing that ridiculous toupee. Nobody, not even Uncle Fred who eats dinner with a shotgun in his lap, would buy a used toupee. Besides, you're a very handsome man. You don't need a toupee. Look at all the attractive balding men in the world. Sean Connery. Bruce Willis. Mr.

Clean. They look great without hair, and so do you.

To: Jausten
From: DaddyO
Subject: No Can Do

Sorry, pumpkin. I'm not giving up my toupee. So what if it smells faintly of tuna? It's a small price to pay for a thick luxurious head of hair.

Your loving,
Daddy

To: Jausten
From: Shoptillyoudrop
Subject: Clear out some drawers

Thanks for trying, honey, but your father still insists on wearing that damn toupee to Cousin Cindy's wedding. My only hope is that the airport security people will detain him for wearing a dead animal on his head.

In the meanwhile, clear out a few drawers for me. It looks like we're going to be roomies.

Your loving,
Mom

PS. You do get the shopping channel, don't you? If not, please order it from your cable company right away.

Chapter

Seventeen

There are definite downsides to living in L.A.: the traffic, the smog, and the inordinate number of women running around in size 2 bikinis.

But on the upside, there's the beach. There's nothing quite like driving west through Santa Monica, past tire shops and gas stations and taco stands, and then suddenly on the horizon, there it is, the Pacific Ocean, glistening in the sun.

I took that drive the next morning, awed as always by the sight of the ocean, then headed south to the tiny beachside community of Ocean Park where Eduardo Jensen lived.

Not that many years ago, Ocean Park was a blighted neighborhood. Its Main Street was a scary place where vagrants loitered in the doorways of industrial buildings. Now it's a hip, trendy place where vagrants loiter in the doorways of latte shops.

I was a half-hour early for my appointment with Eduardo, so I stopped off at one of the latte places and got myself a black coffee and plain bagel. (Okay, so it was a mocha cappuccino and a bagel with cream cheese. Extra cream cheese, if you must know.)

The place was quiet and I nabbed myself a prime seat at the window. As I sat there munching my bagel, I couldn't help worrying about my parents, what with Daddy heading off to Cousin Cindy's wedding in his toupee from hell. But as I told Mom, compared to the rest of the Austen clan, Daddy was the picture of mental health.

No, what really had me worried was the thought of Mom and me becoming "roomies." Mom periodically threatens to move in with me when Daddy's driving her nuts, but Daddy somehow always manages to worm his way back into her good graces. Nevertheless, I live in fear that one day she's going to show up on my doorstep, suitcase in hand, expecting me to stay up all night ordering fake diamonds and polyester pantsuits.

I was halfway through my bagel, wondering if I could fib and tell Mom my cable company didn't carry Home Shopping, when I looked out the window and saw a shabby guy in tattered clothes staring at me. All his worldly possessions were piled into a supermarket cart. His long matted hair hadn't seen a bottle of shampoo in years.

I averted my eyes, and pretended to be looking for something in my purse, hoping that by the time I looked up again, he'd be gone. But, no. When I sneaked a peek out the window, he was still there, staring at me with the same intensity The Blob used to watch Saturday morning cartoons. Suddenly, I lost my appetite. This poor guy was probably starving. I remembered how I'd been mistaken for a vagrant myself the other night, and how miserable that felt. I wrapped up the other half of my bagel, and ordered another to go.

The guy was still there when I got outside, still staring into the latte shop. I tapped him on the shoulder.

"Here," I said, holding out my care package, and trying to ignore his heady aroma of wine and urine.

"What's this?" he asked, eyeing me suspiciously.

"Bagels with cream cheese. I thought you might be hungry."

He looked at me like I'd just handed him one of Tommy the Termite's cockroaches.

"Sorry," he sniffed. "I don't eat dairy

products. Too many toxins."

Welcome to L.A., where even the vagrants eat organic. I swear, if the Statue of Liberty had been built in Los Angeles, its motto would have been: *Give me your tired, your poor, your huddled masses yearning to eat a macrobiotically correct diet.*

Stowing the bagels in my purse, I bid my shabby friend a fond farewell, and headed north a few blocks to the address Eduardo had given me — a cute little $50,000 blue clapboard bungalow now worth close to a million in the maniacally inflated Westside real estate market.

I walked past a picket fence into a tiny front yard and rang the bell. Eduardo answered the door wearing nothing but a towel draped around his waist.

"Sorry," he said, beaming a seductive smile. "I just got out of the shower."

Indeed, his fabulous body glistened with drops of water.

"C'mon in."

He led me into a bright and airy living room. Sleek black-leather-and-chrome furniture stood out in contrast to the bungalow's quaint architectural moldings.

"Make yourself comfy while I get dressed," he said, then padded off down a narrow hallway.

Why did I get the feeling that it was no accident that he'd just stepped out of the shower, that this whole Fabio routine was a ploy to woo potential customers? I could easily picture SueEllen's wealthy girlfriends forking over big bucks for Eduardo's artwork when what they really wanted was his body.

Minutes later he came back, in shorts and a tank top, still doing Fabio.

"Can I get you something to drink?" he asked. "I was just about to make myself a non-dairy tofu-carob-lecithin shake."

"No, thanks," I said, thinking that the bum down on Main Street would probably love some.

He led me into his high tech kitchen, where he tossed a slimy white glob of tofu into a blender. Then he added a raw egg white, some grayish brown carob powder, and the contents of a vitamin capsule.

If that's what it takes to stay healthy, I'd rather die young.

"Sure you don't want some?" he asked, pouring the viscous mixture into a glass. "It's delicious."

"Looks mighty tempting, but I'll pass."

I shuddered as he drank the stuff down in a few gulps.

"Say," he said, wiping away his tofu mustache with the back of his hand, "you ever do any modeling? I'd love to paint you some time."

He flashed me another megawatt smile.

"The only thing I've ever posed for is the photo on my driver's license."

"Maybe some day," he said, huskily, "you'll let me do you."

The guy was about as subtle as a bazooka.

"In the meanwhile, how about we go out to the studio and take a look at my paintings?"

"I can't wait," I lied.

He led me outside past a flagstone patio to his studio, which was housed in a converted garage. Sunlight streamed in through an overhead skylight.

"Voila!" he said, pointing to about a dozen paintings stacked up against the wall.

Holy Moses. I thought I'd died and gone to hell. Every canvas was filled with scenes from your worst nightmare. Dismembered bodies. Fetuses on crucifixes. And a colorful assortment of maggot-ridden corpses. Anyone with a mind this sick, I thought, was capable of throwing a hair dryer into SueEllen's tub.

"So?" he asked. "What do you think?"

I think I'm going to throw up, that's what I think.

"How interesting," I finally managed to croak.

"They make quite a statement," he said.

Yeah. They're saying, "Burn me."

Outside of the contents of an unflushed toilet I'd once stumbled on in Tijuana, never in my life had I seen such nauseating stuff. How the heck was I going to get out of buying one of these monstrosities?

"They're all so wonderful," I chirped, "I'd really like to bring my fiancé back to help me decide."

"Your fiancé?"

"Yes," I lied. Maybe if he thought I had a fiancé, he'd stop doing his Fabio impersonation.

No such luck.

"Why are all the good ones always taken?" he said with a wink.

I followed Eduardo back to his tiny bungalow. My visit was almost over, and I still hadn't managed to work SueEllen into the conversation. I had to say something. And fast.

"I can see why SueEllen was such a big fan of your work," was the best I could come up with.

"Yes, she was," he said, without a trace of modesty.

"Such a tragedy, the way she died."

"A tragedy," he echoed.

By now we were almost at the front door.

"Who on earth would want to kill her?" I asked.

"I have no idea," he said, a note of caution creeping into his voice.

"Do you know that the police suspect Heidi?"

"No, I didn't know. But I'm not surprised, given that scene at her birthday party."

"I don't think Heidi did it," I said. "In fact, I'm sure it was someone else."

"Oh?" he said, his smile frozen.

"I was thinking that maybe somebody had a key to her house, and let himself in while everybody else was gone."

Note the strategic use of the word *himself*.

"Wow," he said, making a big show of checking his watch. "Would you look at the time? I've got to rush to another appointment. You talk it over with your fiancé, and get back to me, okay?"

He held the front door open for me, but I didn't leave.

"Look, Eduardo," I said, abandoning my art lover pose, "I heard SueEllen threatening you the night of Heidi's birthday party."

"Is that so?"

By now his eyes had lost their sexy glint; they were as cold as the chrome on his high tech furniture. Fabio had definitely left the building.

"I was standing outside the poolhouse. I heard everything. SueEllen said she was going to tell everybody about your 'indiscretion,' and that it would ruin your career. And then, the very next day, she died."

His eyes narrowed.

"What are you implying? That I killed SueEllen to keep her from talking?"

"It's an interesting theory."

And then he surprised me. He threw his head back and laughed.

"You're crazy," he said. "Yes, SueEllen was a bitch, and yes, she was threatening to air my dirty laundry in public, but I sure as hell didn't kill her."

"Just how dirty was your laundry?"

"None of your business."

"I know, but tell me anyway."

He laughed again.

"Why not? I've got nothing to hide. The truth is, SueEllen caught me having sex with a teenage girl, the daughter of one of my biggest customers. She was pissed that I'd been cheating on her. SueEllen and I were lovers, but you probably already knew that."

I nodded.

"Everybody knew it," he said, "including her husband, I'll bet. Anyhow, she threatened to tell the girl's mother and everybody else on her Rolodex.

"At first I was panicked. But then, after I thought about it, I calmed down. The kid was eighteen; they couldn't put me in jail. And so what if I lost her mother as a customer? I had plenty more. And it occurred to me that having everyone know I'd been sleeping with a hot young teenager might lend me a certain air of rakish charm.

"So you see," he said, smiling smugly, "I had no reason to kill SueEllen."

"Do you mind my asking where you were the day of the murder?"

"Yeah, I mind. But I'll tell you anyway, just like I told the police. The day Sue-Ellen was killed I was in Santa Barbara, having lunch with a gallery owner. I'll give you his card if you want to call him."

He sounded awfully sure of himself.

"No, that won't be necessary."

"I hope that answers all your questions,"

he said, opening the front door with a flourish.

"Yes, thanks."

I walked out of the bungalow with the uneasy feeling that Eduardo was watching me, and headed back to Main Street where I'd parked the Corolla.

When I reached into my purse for my car keys, I discovered something round and warm and wrapped in tin foil. What a pleasant surprise. It was the bagel and cream cheese I'd bought for Mr. Lactose-Intolerant. I could do with a snack. After all, it had been a whole forty-five minutes since I'd last eaten.

So there I sat behind the steering wheel, munching on my bagel and thinking about my meeting with Eduardo. Those paintings of his were truly disturbing. I had no trouble picturing him as the killer. But according to him, he'd been in Santa Barbara at the time of the murder, and had no real motive to kill SueEllen.

Everything he said made perfect sense. But this is the same guy who said his tofu-carob-lecithin shake was delicious. Which puts a bit of a damper on his believability, don't you think?

I had some time to kill before my appointment with Larkspur, so I stopped off at the bank to deposit Hal's check. And not a moment too soon. My bank balance was so low, the flowers on my designer checks were beginning to wilt. Until I landed another writing assignment, I'd have to be very careful about how I spent my money. I swore to myself I'd make no frivolous purchases, just the bare necessities.

On my way home, I decided to stop off at Bloomingdale's — not to buy anything, of course. No, I only went there because I was hoping to run into Ginny. I wanted to see her reaction when I told her that I knew she'd once been engaged to Hal Kingsley. When I got to the hosiery department, though, she was nowhere in sight. And neither was anybody else. I guess you were out of luck if you wanted to buy socks.

I asked a regal redhead in costume jewelry if Ginny was working that day.

"Yes, she work today," she answered in a thick Russian accent. I had a feeling that at one time in her life, she'd been on the other side of the counter, doing the buying, not the selling. That's the way it is at Bloomingdale's. The place seems to be staffed with women, like Ginny and this

Russian dame, who've fallen on hard times.

"You like this?" she asked, holding up a two hundred dollar crystal and pearl necklace. "It will look marvelous on you, I can tell."

I did like it. A lot. But I couldn't afford it.

"Sorry, no. I don't think so."

"Come on. We just try on. For fun."

But I was strong. No frivolous expenses.

I walked away from the necklace without a backward glance, feeling quite proud of myself.

But as long as I was in Bloomie's, I figured I might as well stop off for a lipstick. I was almost at the bottom of my current tube of Frosted Bronze, and I really needed another. So I headed over to the cosmetics counter, where a woman who looked like she could've been the former Shah-ette of Iran asked if she could help me.

"I need a lipstick," I said, firm in my resolve not to spend a dime more than I had to. "That's all. Just a lipstick."

Twenty minutes later, I walked away with three hundred dollars worth of cosmetics.

I know, I've got the backbone of an egg

noodle. But the Shah-ette swore to me that my Magic Restorative Eye Crème would make my fine lines and wrinkles disappear in a matter of weeks. And the way I saw it, I was saving money. When you think of the thousands of dollars it would have cost to have an eye job from Hal Kingsley, I was actually being very frugal.

Vowing to spend not a penny more, I headed straight for the hosiery department to see if Ginny had returned.

Okay, so I didn't head straight for the hosiery department. I made a quick pit stop at the Eileen Fisher boutique, where I dropped another fifty bucks on a cotton pullover. But once again, I was saving money, since the pullover had been marked down from $135. If I kept this up, I'd be saving thousands of dollars in no time.

Thankfully, I didn't keep it up. I tore myself away from Eileen Fisher and went downstairs to talk to Ginny. But she was still nowhere in sight. Once again, I was reminded of how easy it would have been for her to slip out of the store on her break and drive over to SueEllen's. But if she'd been on her break, wouldn't someone have remembered, and told the police? And wouldn't she have to clock in and out?

These were the questions I mulled as I left the store and headed for the parking garage. But I stopped mulling in front of Tiffany's. Because that's where I saw Ginny coming out of the store, arm in arm with Hal Kingsley.

What the heck had they been doing in Tiffany's? Buying a ring? After twenty-something years, was the engagement back on?

I ducked behind a popcorn kiosk and watched the lovebirds as they headed toward Bloomingdale's. And here's the interesting part. After Hal kissed her goodbye, Ginny walked straight past the employees' entrance and headed back into the store through the customers' door.

So that's how she could've slipped away and murdered SueEllen without anyone knowing. No need to clock in and out. Just use the customers' entrance. With the dearth of sales help in department stores nowadays, no one would even know she'd been gone.

Chapter
Eighteen

An hour later, I was standing in my living room in my bra and panties, humiliated beyond belief as Larkspur O'Leary circled around me, examining my body from all angles. Prozac sat on the sofa, licking her privates and taking in the scene.

"I always like to get a good look at my client's physiology," Larkspur explained, opening the window so the sun could highlight every nook and cranny of my cellulite.

I squirmed uncomfortably, cursing myself for eating those damn bagels. The cream cheese had already taken up permanent residence in my thighs.

"I have a special massage technique that breaks down cellulite," Larkspur said. "That's why I'm so popular."

She stared at my thighs appraisingly, her delicate brows furrowed in what I can only assume was disgust.

"I see we've got our work cut out for us."

I could just hear her now, talking with

her fellow masseuses. *I couldn't believe my eyes. She had cellulite the size of large-curd cottage cheese!*

Then she rummaged through her tote bag and took out a thermos.

"I've brewed you a special tea," she said, pouring me a cup. "I make it for all my clients. It's very relaxing. Drink it while I set up the massage table."

I took a sip. It tasted like rancid tree bark. Not that I know what rancid tree bark tastes like. I'm guessing.

"Drink every drop," she said, as she deftly opened the heavy massage table. For such a tiny thing, she was awfully strong. Strong enough, I wondered, to overpower SueEllen and force her into a deadly bathtub?

I smiled weakly and forced myself to drink the tree bark.

Larkspur spread a fresh sheet on top of the table, and plopped a cassette into a boom box she'd brought with her. Strains of tinkly sitar music filled the air. I don't know about you, but I for one am not a tinkly sitar music fan.

"It's a relaxation tape," she said.

"Very soothing," I lied.

"Now hop on board," she said, patting the massage table.

Easier said than done. After a few futile attempts at hoisting myself up, I finally did it.

Prozac giggled from her perch on the sofa. Okay, so she didn't exactly giggle, but I know she was enjoying this whole humiliating scene.

"You know," Larkspur said, running her finger along my thigh, "you really should avoid dairy products. They're regular cellulite magnets."

Was it my imagination, or was there a vast anti-dairy conspiracy underfoot? First, there was the guy outside the latte shop, then Eduardo with that ghastly non-dairy glop in his blender, and now Larkspur. Was I the only person in greater Los Angeles who still felt any allegiance to Elsie the cow?

"Now roll over on your tummy."

After I rolled, she started slathering a lovely lavender-scented oil on my back. A delicious warmth seeped into my muscles. I was feeling very mellow. But this wasn't the time to be mellow, I reminded myself. I had a suspect to question.

"Such a shame about SueEllen," I threw out for my opening gambit.

Larkspur wasn't having any of it. She put her finger to her rosebud lips, and shushed me.

"No negative thoughts. Otherwise, you won't be totally relaxed."

"Right," I muttered.

"Close your eyes, and imagine yourself on a beach, somewhere in the Caribbean. I hear Jamaica's awfully nice if you don't mind the hostile townspeople. Imagine yourself lying in the sand, the palm trees swaying, cooling you with soft breezes."

I tried imagining myself on the beach, but frankly, all I could think about was how crappy I'd look in a bathing suit with my large-curd cellulite. No doubt about it; one of these days, I was really going to have to lose a few pounds.

In the meanwhile, though, I had a suspect to question. And no idea how to do it. Larkspur clearly didn't want to talk about the murder. How was I going to pump her for information? Why the heck hadn't I worked out a game plan in advance? First I'd wasted time pretending to look at Eduardo's paintings, and now I was throwing away $200 on a massage that was getting me nowhere. I obviously had a lot to learn about the detective biz.

I was feeling quite annoyed with myself when I happened to glance down at Larkspur's open tote bag. And that's when I saw it: a looseleaf binder with the word "appointments" embossed in gold on the cover.

At that moment I knew what I had to do. I had to steal that book.

According to Lt. Webb, Larkspur had been with clients out in Santa Monica the day SueEllen was murdered. He said she wouldn't have had time to drive over to Beverly Hills and toss a hair dryer into SueEllen's tub between appointments. But maybe Larkspur *could* have driven from Santa Monica to Beverly Hills in time to kill SueEllen. It would all depend on traffic, and exactly where in Santa Monica her clients lived. If I could find out where Larkspur's appointments were on the day of the murder, I could do a test run, and drive the distance myself.

Yes, I'd have to steal the book. The question, of course, was how.

And then I thought of an absolutely brilliant idea. I'd pretend I was having a hypoglycemic attack and send Larkspur into the kitchen to get me some apple juice. Then, while she was in the kitchen, I'd hide the book under one of the sofa cushions. I'd seen a similar plan on an old episode of *Three's Company*, the one where Jack is trying to get rid of Mr. Roper so he won't discover the chimpanzee he's got hidden in the hall closet. Okay, so maybe it wasn't brilliant, but it was all I could think of at the time.

True, I didn't have hypoglycemia — or apple juice, either. But it didn't matter. By the time Larkspur got back to the living room, I'd pretend I was feeling better. Then, after she'd gone, I'd pore over her book and find out the names of her clients and do my test run. Maybe I'd even solve the murder, stunning the cops with my investigative acumen.

Now all I had to do was wait for the massage to be over. After all, it was costing me two hundred bucks; I might as well get my money's worth. I closed my eyes, wondering if Larkspur really could get rid of my cellulite. Wouldn't it be great if she could? I let my mind drift to that Caribbean beach she'd been talking about. I saw myself walking along the shoreline in a string bikini, my thighs as smooth and silky as hot fudge sauce. Then, just as I was making smoldering eye contact with a bronzed cabana boy, I heard Larkspur chirp:

"All done!"

"That's impossible," I said. "You just started."

"No," she said, "it's been almost an hour."

I checked my wristwatch. She was right. It *had* been almost an hour.

"You fell asleep."

"I did?"

"It's the tea," she said, nodding. "It's very relaxing. Lots of my clients fall asleep."

And then I realized: I didn't have to go through my phony hypoglycemic attack. I didn't have to steal the appointment book, or question Larkspur's clients, or do any test drives from Santa Monica to Beverly Hills.

Because I already knew how Larkspur could have killed SueEllen.

She could have drugged her client with her tree bark tea. Then she could have moseyed over to SueEllen's and tossed the hair dryer in the tub, knowing she had all the time in the world — because her client was sound asleep on the massage table, dreaming of cellulite-free thighs.

I barely contained my impatience as Larkspur packed up her things.

"Remember," she said. "Stay away from dairy products. And caffeine!"

Then she whipped out her appointment book and asked if I'd like to schedule another massage. I told her I'd get back to her. Yeah, right. I'd get back to her. When

Oreos weren't fattening, that's when I'd get back to her.

The minute she was gone, I dashed to the phone, and called Lt. Webb.

"What is it now?" was his cordial opening line.

"I've got news for you," I said. "Larkspur O'Leary's alibi isn't as ironclad as you think it is."

"Hold on a sec," he said, then shouted out to somebody else in the room. "I want the ahi nicoise salad and a Diet Coke. And make sure the ahi is rare."

Our tax dollars at work.

"You were saying?" he said, grudgingly turning his attention back to me.

"I know how Larkspur could have killed SueEllen."

"Is that so?"

And I told him about the tea.

"Well, I've got news for you, too," he said when I was through.

My heart sank; something in his voice told me it wasn't going to be good news.

"Apparently the Kingsleys had their carpets cleaned today."

So far, not exactly earthshattering.

"And guess what the cleaning crew found stuffed away in the back of Heidi's closet?"

"What?"

"A blond wig."

Damn.

"Looks like we found our mysterious blonde," he said.

"Oh, come on. You don't really think Heidi's the blonde in the bathroom."

"Yeah, I do."

"It doesn't make sense. Why would she leave the wig in her closet for the cops to find? Why didn't she just throw it away in a trash can?"

"Maybe she figured we had undercover cops following her round the clock. Which we did."

Gulp.

"Better tell your client to hold off on her college applications. It looks like she'll be spending the next four years making license plates."

He hung up without bothering to say goodbye. I wanted to strangle the guy. He'd already tried and convicted Heidi without the benefit of a jury.

The receiver was still warm when the phone rang again. It was Heidi, her voice choked with tears.

"Oh, Jaine, the most awful thing has happened."

"I know all about it. I'll be right over."

I grabbed my car keys, and hurried out to the Corolla.

By now, of course, you're probably wondering if maybe Heidi *could* have done it. True confession: I wondered the same thing. For maybe three seconds. But I knew in my heart the kid was innocent. Anyone could have planted that wig in her closet on the day of SueEllen's memorial service. All my suspects were there: Larkspur, Ginny, Denise, and Eduardo. Not to mention Hal and Brad. Any one of them could have slipped upstairs, just as I had, without being noticed. Any one of them could have wandered along the hallway till they found Heidi's hot pink bedroom, and dropped off their incriminating package.

I slogged through rush hour traffic and finally made it to Casa Kingsley.

Conchi opened the door, clutching her Windex bottle to her chest, a security blanket with Ammonia-D. She had that scared rabbit look in her eyes, like maybe she thought the immigration guys had finally caught up with her.

When she saw it was me, she sighed with relief.

"Thank God, it's you," she said. "I thought you were the police. Those *diablos*. They won't leave my poor Heidi alone."

She led me to the den, the scene of my famous macadamia nut hunt. Heidi was sitting on the sofa, being comforted by Grandma Kosciusko.

"Hey, kiddo," I said.

She looked up at me, her face red and blotchy from crying.

"It's not my wig, Jaine. I swear."

"I know, honey," I said, hurrying to her side.

"I don't know how it got there."

"Somebody put it there," I said, "and I'm going to find out who."

Spoken as if I actually knew what I was doing.

Grandma K's eyes widened with dismay. "You don't really think somebody's trying to frame Heidi for SueEllen's murder?"

"I'm afraid I do."

"What sort of monster would do such a thing?"

I had a list of suspects two pages long. And one of them was her own son. But I wasn't about to tell her that.

"You really think you can find the killer?"

"I'll try my best."

Who did I think I was kidding? I hadn't had an ounce of success so far. What Heidi needed was a real detective. Where was

Kinsey Millhone when you needed her?

Grandma K looked like she'd aged five years in the past two days.

"It's all my fault," she moaned. "If only I hadn't called the carpet cleaners. The carpets weren't even that dirty."

At which point, Conchi scuttled in the room with a plate of fresh baked cookies.

"Here, Miss Heidi," she said. "Chocolate chip. Your favorite."

"Thanks, Conchi." Heidi wiped away her tears with the back of her hand. "But I'm not hungry."

Conchi set the cookies down on the coffee table. "Maybe you'll have one later." Then she scuttled back out of the room, muttering *Ay, caramba! Dios Mio,* or words to that effect.

Maybe Heidi wasn't hungry, but I'm ashamed to say I was. Those cookies looked fabulous. I barely restrained myself from reaching out and grabbing one. Okay, so I didn't restrain myself. I took one.

Okay, I took two.

Heidi turned to me with red-rimmed eyes.

"What if they arrest me?"

"They're not going to arrest you," Hal said, striding into the room, tall and cool and confident. "I just got off the phone

267

with my attorneys."

Attorneys, plural. Hal wasn't taking any chances. He sat down next to Heidi and took her in his arms. "Nothing's going to happen to you, sweetheart. I promise."

At last, he was showing her some affection.

I left Heidi in the arms of her father and headed out to my Corolla. It was a very touching scene I'd just witnessed. Maybe with Grandma K around, Hal was turning into a human being again.

But then again, maybe he wasn't. There was a cynical voice inside my head scripting another scenario: Maybe Hal had indeed killed SueEllen. But he knew he couldn't afford to be a suspect, not even for a minute. His whole medical practice was at stake. Maybe he figured it wouldn't matter so much if the cops suspected Heidi. After all, she was a kid. She had no reputation to ruin. In two years, the whole thing would be forgotten.

Was it possible that Hal Kingsley had framed his own daughter for a crime he committed, confident that he could get her off the hook with a dream team of lawyers?

Chapter
Nineteen

It was dark when I stepped outside onto the Kingsleys' circular driveway. The fog was rolling in, and so was Brad. He came roaring up the driveway in his Ferrari, leaving a fine spray of gravel in his wake. His car stereo was blaring a delightful rap tune. Something about a guy getting it on with his fat-assed bitch.

Eat your heart out, Irving Berlin.

Brad mercifully turned off the ignition and hopped out of the car, whistling a happy tune, not a care in the world. Until he saw me standing there, arms folded across my chest. Then he didn't look so happy.

"Hey, Judy."

"It's Jaine."

"Right," he smirked. "Jane Eyre. Like the author."

Why did I get the feeling that he knew exactly what my name was?

"Mind if I ask you a question?" I forced myself to smile.

"Shoot," he said.

"Doesn't it bother you that the cops suspect your sister of murder? Aren't you worried that she might wind up in jail?"

"Nah," he said, dismissing my fears with a wave of his hand. "Dad'll take care of everything."

Spoken with the confidence of a kid who knew he could break the law and get away with it.

"Lt. Webb tells me you were on your lunch break at the time of SueEllen's murder."

"That's right," he said. "And I've got three friends who'll back me up."

"I'm sure they will. That's what friends are for, right?"

That wiped the smirk off his face.

"Screw you," he muttered cordially, then turned on his heels and headed back to the house.

What a rotten kid. I felt like keying his Ferrari.

Instead I got in my Corolla and started home.

I could easily picture Brad Kingsley killing SueEllen for a Ferrari, and then framing his sister for the murder. So what if his friends swore he was with them at the time SueEllen was killed? They could be lying to cover for him. If they were anything like Brad, they had the ethics of a gerbil.

Between Brad, Hal, and my bevy of blondes, my mind was reeling with suspects. What I needed was a relaxing soak in the tub, where I could lie back and sort things out. I'd been avoiding the tub, after seeing SueEllen electrocuted in hers. But I had to get over that silly fear. Tonight, I was definitely going to make a return appearance in my bathtub.

In the meanwhile, I stopped off to pick up something nutritious for dinner. I remembered Larkspur's advice about staying away from dairy products. So I told the clown I wouldn't be having a milkshake with my Jumbo Jack and fries.

My answering machine was blinking when I got home. One whole message. It's a good thing I had that five thousand dollars from Hal. I sure as heck wasn't getting any writing jobs.

It was Kandi.

Well, sweetie. I think this could be the night. Matt's taking me to dinner at the beach. He said he had an important question he wanted to ask me. I smell an engagement ring! I know what you're thinking, that we've only been out on three dates, but I'm telling you, Jaine, this guy is Mr. Right. Did I mention that he can bench press four hundred pounds? And he cracks walnuts with his bare hands. Not that I eat walnuts; they're so damn fattening. The point is, Matt's the strong, silent type of guy I should have been dating all along. So wish me luck tonight. Oh, and before I forget. Major news flash about Tommy the Termite. Apparently he got caught by a health inspector dropping a cockroach into a barbeque chicken pizza. It'll be in the trades tomorrow. "Toon Termite Caught Bugging." We're going to have to write him out of the series. It'll be a very special episode. Tommy the Termite Meets the Orkin Man. Okay, honey. Gotta run. Love you.

I shook my head, amused and amazed. I didn't know which was more impressive: Kandi's eternal optimism or her ability to leave the world's longest phone messages.

But I did wish her luck. "Who knows?" I said to Prozac. "Maybe this bench-pressing, walnut-cracking guy really is Mr. Right."

Prozac meowed angrily, as if to say, *Who cares about Kandi? Can't you get your priorities straight? It's time for my dinner.*

So I padded into the kitchen and opened her a can of yummy chicken innards. I was

272

just unwrapping my Jumbo Jack when the phone rang in the living room. I hurried to get it.

It was Morris Pechter, Mrs. Pechter's adorable grandson. His voice was soft, and a little shy. I'm a sucker for shy.

"Grandma Rose gave me your phone number."

I just loved the way he called Mrs. Pechter *Grandma Rose*.

"Anyhow, I was hoping we could have dinner. Maybe Friday night?"

I told him that Friday night sounded just marvelous, and we agreed that he'd pick me up around eight.

I hung up, smiling. I remembered what Mrs. Pechter wrote in her essay, about how Morris took her to dinner once a week. Such a sweet thing to do. That made me like him all the more. And the fact that he looked a bit like Hugh Grant didn't hurt either.

I hurried back to the kitchen for my Jumbo Jack. It had been ages since I'd wolfed down my bagels and cream cheese and I was starving.

I know, a fast food burger is loaded with fat, and I really shouldn't have been eating one. And as it turns out, I didn't. Because by the time I got back to the kitchen,

Prozac was up on the counter, her little pink nose burrowing into my Jumbo Jack, practically inhaling it.

"Prozac!" I shrieked. "How could you?"

She looked up at me briefly, then went back to burrowing.

Frankly, I couldn't blame her. I'm sure it was a lot tastier than her chicken innards. So I poured myself a glass of chardonnay, and sat down to a hearty dinner of ketchup and fries. For dessert, I had a pickle slice Prozac was kind enough to leave untouched.

Then I went into my bedroom and got undressed. It was time for my bath. I swept aside my uneasy feelings about venturing back into the tub. I really needed some serious soaking time to think about my suspects. I slipped on my robe and headed for the bathroom to run the water for my bath.

When I opened the door, I froze in my tracks.

There was no need for me to run the water. Somebody had already done it for me. The tub was filled to the brim.

And floating on the surface of the water was my hair dryer. Plugged in, and ready to electrocute.

Chapter Twenty

Clearly I'd just received a love note from the killer: *Lay off, or you're next.* The important thing, I told myself, was not to panic. Absolutely, do not panic. And so, naturally, I proceeded to panic. Big time.

I ran screaming into the bedroom and banged on the wall.

"Lance! Are you there?"

No answer.

Damn. He was probably on a date with Jim. He had some nerve going out and enjoying himself in my moment of crisis.

And then I remembered Prozac. Poor darling Prozac! What if, while I was in the bedroom, banging on the wall, she'd decided to abandon thousands of years of genetic programming and leaped in the tub? I dashed back into the bathroom, half expecting to see her furry little body floating lifeless next to the hair dryer. But of course, she wasn't there; she was back in the living room, belching Jumbo Jack fumes.

Thank goodness she was safe. I raced back to the bathroom, and shut the door so she couldn't get in.

Meanwhile, what on earth was I going to do about the hair dryer? Did I have to turn off the circuit breaker for the whole apartment, or could I just unplug it? I was sure there were emergency directions on the electrical cord of the dryer, but I couldn't read them because the dryer was in the tub. So I did what any rational person would do:

I called 911.

The dispatcher wasn't exactly thrilled to hear from me.

"Somebody filled your tub with water? That's not exactly an emergency, Ma'am."

She told me that 911 was for medical emergencies and crimes in progress, and advised me to hang up and call my local police station.

They weren't all that thrilled to hear from me either.

"Someone broke in to my apartment!"

"Did they take anything, Ma'am?"

"No, but they put a hair dryer in my tub."

"A hair dryer in your tub?" I heard him stifle a yawn. "You want us to send someone out there?"

"Of course, I want you to send someone."

"I only ask because there was no actual burglary."

"Don't you understand? Someone put a hair dryer into a tub full of water."

"Are you sure it didn't fall in by accident? That happens all the time, you know."

"No," I said, with forced calm, "it didn't fall in by accident."

I gave him my address and slammed down the phone. Then I called Lt. Webb, who was gone for the day. Probably out somewhere making sure his sashimi was fresh. I left him a message, telling him about my death-threat hair dryer, and asked him to get in touch with me as soon as possible.

Then I did what I should have done in the first place. I drank my glass of chardonnay.

Forty-five minutes and another glass of chardonnay later, two bored cops rang my doorbell. Unlike the Marlboro men who showed up at the Kingsleys, these two were from the low rent division of the Beverly Hills Police Department. One was a tall, skinny, freckle-faced kid, whose name was Officer Mason. The other was big and beefy with muscles the size of hamhocks. Her name was Officer Schmitt. Prozac took one look at her and dove under the sofa.

I ushered the cops to the bathroom, and showed them the tub.

"Somebody broke into my apartment and did this."

The cops looked at the empty wine glass in my hand, and exchanged glances.

"Are you sure you didn't fill the tub yourself, and then forgot about it?" the beefy one asked.

Oh, God. They thought I was drunk.

"No, I didn't fill the tub myself. And I didn't drop the hair dryer in there, either."

"Maybe it fell in by accident," the skinny one said, pulling the plug from the socket.

"Don't you understand? This is a death threat. Whoever did this wants me to call off my investigation into SueEllen Kingsley's murder."

The cops exchanged another glance.

"Whatever you say, Ma'am."

Clearly these two had me pegged as a drunken kookoo so desperate for attention, I reported make-believe death threats.

"I swear, I did not do this myself. For the umpteenth time, somebody broke into my apartment."

"There are no signs of forced entry, Ma'am. We checked before we rang your bell."

"But look. The living room window is open."

"Are you sure you didn't leave it open yourself?"

And then I remembered that Larkspur had opened it to let the sun shine on my cellulite. In my haste to get over to Heidi's today, I'd forgotten to close it.

"Okay, so maybe I did leave it open, but I want you to dust for fingerprints. It's my unalienable right as a Beverly Hills citizen!"

The beefy one looked at me, and sighed.

"You want my advice, honey? Lay off the sauce."

They opened the front door to leave, but they didn't get very far, because standing there in the doorway was Lt. Webb. Very tall, very imposing, very Clint Eastwood.

Prozac, the little slut, crept out from under the sofa and trotted over to him, rubbing his ankles with wild abandon. She has a thing for hunky authority figures.

"I got your message," he said, sidestepping Prozac's shameless advances. Then he flashed his badge at the two cops. They snapped to attention.

"Good evening, sir," the beefy one said.

"Show me the crime scene," he commanded.

Good heavens. He said *crime scene*. Did that mean he was actually taking me seriously?

We trooped back to the bathroom, and watched the hair dryer floating in the tub.

"It was plugged in when I found it," I said.

"I unplugged it," the skinny one piped up, eager to claim credit.

"Bully for you," Webb said. "Now talk to the neighbors and find out if they saw anybody entering the building."

"Yes, sir," he said, practically saluting.

"And you," Webb said to the beefy one. "You dust for prints."

I shot her a *ha ha, so there!* look as she left the room.

"This was obviously a warning," Lt. Webb said when we were alone. "Somebody wants you to mind your own business."

"It wasn't you, was it?" I joked.

But he didn't crack a smile; he was still doing Eastwood.

"You can't possibly think it's Heidi, can you?" I asked. "She's been begging me to stay on the case, not off."

"Nope. It's not the kid. Like I told you, we've had a tail on her for days. She didn't come anywhere near here today. And we tested the wig in her closet. Didn't match any of the hairs we found in SueEllen's bathroom."

Thank heavens. For the first time since we met, it looked like he thought Heidi might be innocent.

"I'm going to question some of the neighbors myself," he said. "You sit tight."

Which is exactly what I did. Me, and my third glass of chardonnay.

An hour later, the prints were dusted and the neighbors were questioned. Nobody saw anyone breaking into my building.

But one old man walking his dog did see a woman heading up the front path to my apartment. He didn't pay much attention to her. All he could remember was that she was a blonde.

Officers Mason and Schmitt packed up their dusting kit, and headed back to the police station. I could tell they thought the whole thing had been a waste of time. But that didn't stop them from bowing and scraping to Lt. Webb on their way out.

Webb stowed the hair dryer in one of

those plastic evidence bags. Maybe some day it would be Exhibit "A" in the Sue-Ellen Kingsley murder trial.

He looked at me with steely gray eyes.

"Take my advice, Jaine. Lay off the case. Whoever killed SueEllen won't have any qualms about killing you."

Maybe he was right. Maybe it was time for me to mind my own business, and let the cops handle things. Finding that dryer in the tub had put the fear of God in me. But what if it was too late? What if I'd gone too far?

"What if the killer comes back tonight?" I asked.

"Don't worry," Webb assured me. "That probably won't happen."

I didn't like the way he said "probably."

I spent the rest of the night barricaded in my bedroom with Prozac, who, as she always does in my times of need, demanded a belly rub. After which, she jumped off the bed and curled up on my dresser. I'd serviced her, and now she had no further use for me.

"One of these days," I threatened, "I'm going to get a loveable poodle who'll steal my heart and eat your cat food."

She just yawned and licked her privates. Sometimes I think that cat has the cleanest genitalia in feline history.

Sleep was impossible. I tried watching TV, but that was a bust.

Have you ever noticed how every time you're worried about something and you try and watch TV to escape, the thing you're worried about inevitably shows up on the screen? Like if you've just had a Pap smear, and you're worried about the results, and then you turn on the TV, and there on the news is a story about a Pap smear lab that got all the test results mixed up.

That night, I turned on the TV, hoping to find a nice escapist movie. Instead I found a Women in Jeopardy film festival. It seemed like everywhere I looked some beautiful but helpless woman was being stalked by a crazed killer. I gave up on the movies, and tried the shopping channel, but they were doing one of their Lethal Knives shows. Next, I switched to CSPAN, normally the epitome of bland, only to find a sociology professor talking about famous serial killers in history. With glorious technicolor pictures of their bloodied victims.

At last I found an infomercial for an acne medication. It wasn't exactly riveting television, but at least nobody died a violent death.

Eventually — somewhere in the middle of an infomercial for a pot that cooked entire meals while its owners were out frolicking on the beach — Prozac crawled back in bed, and curled up against the crook of my neck. Only then was I able to drift off into a fitful sleep.

Chapter
Twenty-One

I woke up the next day, feeling like a used Q-Tip.

I briefly considered taking a shower, but I didn't want to use the bathroom any longer than I absolutely had to. Which is why I wound up brushing my teeth at the kitchen sink.

I threw on a pair of my grungiest sweats and checked myself out in the mirror. I had bags under my eyes the size of carry-on luggage. And my hair, thanks to a sweaty night tossing and turning, had blossomed into a glorious bush of Brillo. All I needed was a supermarket cart filled with my worldly possessions, and I'd be sharing a doorway with my lactose-intolerant buddy in Ocean Park.

After feeding Prozac a gourmet breakfast of mackerel guts, I decided to drive out to the beach. Maybe a walk on the sand would clear my head.

On my way out to the Corolla, I ran into Lance, who was walking up the path to his apartment. He was positively glowing, probably from a night of whoopsy doodle with Jim.

"You'll never guess where I was all night," he beamed.

"Chained to a bed, with velvet-lined handcuffs?"

"How'd you know?" He giggled. "Seriously, Jaine, it was heaven. I don't think I've ever known what love was like until now. Sex, yes. But not love."

Is there anything more nauseating than a friend in the first gooey stages of infatuation? I could practically feel my blood turn to sugar.

"That's great, Lance."

"Hey," he said. "What happened to you? You look terrible."

"Thanks for noticing."

"No, really. What happened?"

"Actually, I got a death threat last night."

"Omigod. That's awful. You know, Jim once got a death threat when a house he sold turned out to be riddled with mold."

"Right," I said. "Well, gotta run. See you later."

He waved goodbye and sailed into his apartment, still basking in the afterglow of frantic sex.

After a quick pit stop for an Egg McMuffin, I took Santa Monica Boulevard out to the Coast Highway, then headed north to Will Rogers State Beach. It was an overcast day, gray and raw.

I parked my car in the public lot, and rummaged through my glove compartment for an old screwdriver I kept there in case of an auto emergency. I don't know what I thought I was going to fix with a screwdriver, since I had trouble figuring out how to open the hood of my car, but I kept it there anyway.

Now I was glad I had it. Thinking it would make a good self-defense weapon in case the killer was following me, I put it in my pocket and headed out onto the sand.

The usual fitness freaks were there, doing their daily runs, working off every possible ounce of fat from their bodies.

I set out on a brisk walk. The cold air felt good against my face.

I'd gone to bed last night convinced that I should take Lt. Webb's advice and lay off the case. But as I walked along the shoreline, the sand crunching beneath my feet, yesterday's panic gradually turned to anger. Someone was trying to intimidate me. And I didn't like it.

Then I thought of Daddy and his stubborn refusal to give up his ridiculous toupee. I guess I must have inherited his stubborn genes. Because I knew then and there that I wasn't going to give in. I wasn't going to go crawling back to my computer, my tail between my legs, and start churning out Toiletmasters brochures. No, I'd started this case, and I'd damn well finish it. The fact that I hadn't the faintest clue who the killer was was a tad unsettling, but I wasn't going to let that stop me. I was strong! I was invincible! I was —

Damn. I was covered with sand.

A kamikaze runner with a dog the size of a Chrysler Cruiser had just zoomed past me, kicking up wet globs of sand onto my sweats.

"Get tendonitis!" I shouted after him.

I wiped myself off and continued walking.

I thought back to the hair dryer floating in my tub last night, and wondered who put it there.

The first person who sprung to mind was Brad. The very act of filling my tub with water and tossing in a hair dryer seemed like a prank, something a high school kid would do. But it couldn't have been Brad. The neighbor across the street said the person he saw was a blonde.

So I was back to the blondes. Had Larkspur realized that she'd made a slip when she told me about her sleep-inducing tea? Frightened that I'd go to the cops, did she sneak back to my apartment to leave me a little warning note? Or had Hal sent Denise to do the dirty deed? And of course, there was Ginny. As much as I didn't want to believe it, it was possible she'd killed SueEllen to get her old boyfriend back, and then dropped the hair dryer in my tub when I was getting close to figuring out what she'd done.

Any one of them could have done it. And yet, I couldn't let go of my Teenage Prank theory. And that's when I remembered Brad's girlfriend Amber, or — as I preferred to think of her — Bathtub Barbie.

Was she the one who strolled up my path last night? Had she been acting on Brad's orders? Was Brad sitting out in the Ferrari waiting for her while she dropped the dryer in my tub?

Nah, I didn't think so. Amber wasn't the kind of girl to take chances for somebody else. The only person Amber would risk her neck for was Amber.

Then I remembered what Eduardo said

about having an affair with a teenager. What if he was telling the truth, and that young girl was Amber? Hadn't I seen her flirting with him at Heidi's birthday party?

And what if it hadn't been Brad she'd been waiting for that night in the bathtub — but Eduardo? What if they were having an affair and SueEllen found out about it? Then, when SueEllen threatened to tell Amber's mom, maybe Amber killed her to shut her up.

An interesting theory, all right. Now all I had to do was prove it.

I was feeling quite proud of my Sherlock Holmesian powers of deduction when I abruptly found myself ankle-deep in water. I'd been so busy playing detective, I hadn't noticed a wave breaking high on the shore. My feet were soaked. I bet this kind of stuff never happened to Sherlock.

Luckily I was wearing a pair of ratty old tennis shoes. I plucked the seaweed from my sweatpants and straggled back up to the Corolla. Then I turned on the heater and headed south to Ocean Park. As long as I was at the beach, I might as well swing by Eduardo's to see if I could find out if Amber was, indeed, his teenage lover.

I found a parking spot on Main Street, and made my way to Eduardo's bungalow, my sneakers squishing with every step. I showed up just in time to see a woman in sexy capris and a tight spandex T-shirt walking inside. Her back was toward me, so I couldn't see her face.

I could see her hair, though. It was sleek and shiny.

And blond.

I watched the blonde disappear inside the bungalow, my heart racing. Something told me I had just stumbled onto SueEllen's killer.

Much to my disappointment, it didn't look like Amber. From what I'd seen of Amber in the bathtub, she wore a size 2, max. This gal had a bit more meat on her bones. Could it be Larkspur? Ginny? Denise? Could one of them have been partners with Eduardo in a plot to kill SueEllen?

Maybe it was some other blonde I didn't even know about. The world seemed to be teeming with blondes who wanted SueEllen out of the way. Or maybe my heart was racing in vain. Maybe it was just one of Eduardo's many lovers, come for a mid-morning tryst.

I had to find out.

Ringing the doorbell was out of the

question. Eduardo was sure to turn me away. So I crept around the side of the house, my sneakers still squishing. I only hoped they couldn't hear me inside.

I peered in the living room, but it was empty. So I continued on past a tiny den. Empty, too. Then, at the back of the house, much to my annoyance, I saw that the windows were set high up on the wall. Damn. I couldn't even begin to see in. I looked around and saw some empty terracotta planters by the fence separating Eduardo's property from his neighbor's. I grabbed the largest of the lot and turned it upside down under the window. Then I stepped on it gingerly, hoping it would hold me. My thighs and I are happy to report that it did.

I looked inside the window into what was obviously Eduardo's bedroom. A king-sized bed with black satin sheets dominated the room. And stretched out on those sheets, alone in the room, was the blonde. Probably waiting for Eduardo to gather his sex toys and ravish her.

At last, I could see her face. It wasn't any of the usual suspects. Not Ginny. Not Larkspur. Not Denise. But there was something about her that looked familiar.

Then slowly, languorously, she reached

up to her beautiful blond hair — and pulled it off. Good Lord, she was wearing a wig. And Good Lord, Part II — it wasn't a She. It was a He. It was Eduardo! No wonder that face looked familiar.

He got up from the bed and started undressing. And I'm ashamed to say, I watched. I couldn't help myself. He kicked off his high heels, then peeled off his capris and tank top. Underneath he was wearing a black lace bra and panty set, straight out of Victoria's Secret Extra Naughty Department. Except for the bulge in his black lace panties, he made a damn convincing woman.

I watched as he reached into his bra and pulled out a pair of sweat socks. When he started to take off the panties, I called it a day and got down off the planter, stunned at what I'd just seen. Eduardo Jensen was a transvestite. That was the dirty secret SueEllen threatened to tell the world. Not that he was boffing a young girl, but that he was dressing like one.

And that's why he killed her. He couldn't let her destroy his reputation as a stud-about-town. So he put on his blond wig, sashayed down the hallway to her bathroom, and tossed a hair dryer in her tub.

I'd bet my Joan & David suede boots that the hairs from his wig would match the hairs found at the murder scene. I had to call Lt. Webb right away. But what if Eduardo destroyed the wig before the cops could confiscate it? What if he'd worn it this morning one last time, for old time's sake, and was planning to toss it in his trash compactor? I couldn't take any chances. I'd have to get it myself. I'd simply break into the house, grab the wig and —

"What the hell are you doing here?"

It was Eduardo, in shorts and a tank top, all traces of his makeup washed away.

He was smiling, an icy smile that turned my palms slick with sweat.

"Oh, hi, Eduardo." My voice was a frightened squeak. "I came back to buy one of your paintings. I talked it over with my fiancé, and we thought the one with the dead fetus would look great over our fireplace."

I took a step backwards, but he grabbed my arm. He was much stronger than he looked.

"Nice try," he said, still smiling that icy smile, "but I don't believe you."

"No, really. I rang the bell but I guess it isn't working. I figured you were in your studio so I came around the side of the house."

He looked down at the planter, then up at the window.

"You saw me, didn't you?"

"I don't know what you're talking about."

He tightened his painful grip on my arm.

"I guess you must know my little secret."

"What little secret? I came here to buy a painting."

"Okay then, why don't we go out to the studio?" he said, dragging me towards his garage.

Oh, God. I thought of all those awful paintings, the dead fetuses, the disemboweled corpses. This was a sick man.

"We've got a problem here," he said, yanking me along, "and we've got to solve it. I can't have you telling the world the truth about me, can I?"

I started to scream, but he clamped his hand over my mouth. I could smell faint traces of perfume on his wrist.

Why hadn't I listened to Lt. Webb? Why hadn't I given up on this ridiculous investigation and minded my own business? I could've killed myself for being such a jerk, only I had a feeling Eduardo was about to do it for me.

"What's going on here?"

I looked up and saw two cops coming towards us.

Reluctantly, Eduardo let go of me.

"Thank God you've come!" I said, practically hurling myself into their arms.

For those of you keeping track of the many police officers who seemed to be cropping up in my life, these two were named Washington and Ramirez. Ramirez was a tough looking Hispanic guy, and Washington was an even tougher looking black woman. She made Officer Schmitt look like Calista Flockheart.

"Am I glad to see you," Eduardo said, his icy smile turning cordial. "This woman was trying to break into my house."

"That's what we thought," Ramirez said. "The lady next door reported a burglary in progress. Said someone was trying to climb in the back window."

Great. Just great. Where was this lady yesterday while someone was climbing in *my* window?

"That's right," Eduardo said. "I apprehended her, and I was just about to call 911."

"That's not true!" I cried. "He was just about to kill me, that's what he was about to do. This man is a killer!"

"Don't be absurd," Eduardo said, doing a great job of looking outraged.

"It's true! He killed SueEllen Kingsley. He's the blonde Heidi saw in the hallway. He's the one who dropped the hair dryer in SueEllen's tub. And last night he dropped one in my tub. And just now, he was going to take me into his studio with all those ghastly pictures and kill me. You wouldn't believe the awful pictures he's got in there. Really. Why anyone would pay good money for those monstrosities, I'll never know —"

Why was I rambling like this? I sounded like a nutcase.

I guess that's what the cops thought, because the next thing I knew I was standing up against the wall with my legs spread. Then Officer Washington started frisking me, touching me in places that only The Blob and my gynecologist had gone before.

I craned my neck to make eye contact with Ramirez. Maybe he'd be more sympathetic.

"I swear, officer. I'm not a burglar."

"That's not what the lady next door says. She saw you trying to break in this window."

"I wasn't breaking in, I was looking in. There's a big difference. And okay, maybe

I was thinking of breaking in, but only because I didn't want him destroying evidence!"

"Look what I found," Washington said.

She held up my screwdriver.

"She was probably going to use it to jimmy open the window."

"No! I was using it to protect myself, in case the killer attacked me."

They exchanged "loony alert" looks, much like the looks I was getting last night from the Beverly Hills cops.

Eduardo shook his head, pityingly.

"Just another drug addict looking for a quick fix," he said. "The neighborhood is full of them."

"Better cuff her," Ramirez said.

"You don't understand —"

"We understand," Washington said, slapping a pair of handcuffs on my wrists. "We understand you're going to jail."

Grabbing me by the elbows, they escorted me out to their squad car. Ramirez was nice enough to read me my rights en route.

Eduardo shouted his thanks to the cops, then headed back inside.

"You've got to believe me. I'm a private investigator."

They had a good chuckle over that one.

"Oh, yeah? Let's see your license."

"I don't exactly have a license, but I'm investigating the SueEllen Kingsley murder."

By now, Washington was on the phone, reporting to headquarters.

"Suspect apprehended. Probably a junkie looking for drug money."

A junkie? What on earth would make them think I was a junkie?

And then I saw my reflection in the window of the squad car. Of course, they thought I was a junkie. I was dressed in my ratty sweats, which, thanks to that kamikaze runner, were clotted with sand. My hair was wild and I reeked of seaweed. Not exactly a profile of your law abiding citizen.

"I swear on a stack of bibles, I'm not a junkie. I really am investigating a murder. And the man in that house is a killer."

"Yeah, right," Washington said. "And I'm Mike Tyson."

I didn't want to say anything, but she did bear a vague resemblance to him.

"Don't you understand? The minute we leave, he's going to destroy the wig and our only shred of evidence will be gone."

"Obviously on hallucinogens," Ramirez said, shaking his head.

"Don't worry," Washington said, as she shoved me into the back seat of the squad car. "You'll sleep it off in a nice comfy jail cell."

Chapter
Twenty-Two

I begged the cops to call Lt. Webb to verify my story, but they refused.

"Call him yourself," was Officer Washington's helpful suggestion.

Which is exactly what I did after being fingerprinted and booked at the Van Nuys jail. For those of you gals planning to get arrested in West Los Angeles, that's where they take you, all the way out to scenic Van Nuys, the Used Car Lot Capital of the World.

I can't tell you how humiliating it was riding out there on the freeway, handcuffed in the back seat of the squad car like some sort of criminal. Which, of course, we both know I wasn't.

What really steamed me was that scads of people were zooming past us, breaking the speed limit by at least ten miles per hour, while I — who never ever go beyond the speed limit, mainly because my Corolla has the horsepower of Mr. Ed — was the one being carted off to jail.

When they finally let me use the phone, I called Lt. Webb, but just my luck, he wasn't in. I left a frantic message on his voice mail about Eduardo's wig and my ignominious arrest, and begged him to call Van Nuys and explain to the cops that I was not a felon, but an innocent writer-detective.

I later found out that Lt. Webb's six-year-old boy had fallen off a jungle gym and was rushed to the emergency room with a nasty cut. Lt. Webb had gone to be at his side while the kid got stitches. Which, I have to confess, surprised me. Not that the kid got stitches, but the fact that Lt. Webb even had a kid. Somehow I didn't picture Lt. Webb with a family. I pictured him living alone in a sparsely furnished condo with nothing for company except a bottle of scotch and a Soloflex machine.

But the point is, he did have a little boy, and he had rushed to the emergency room. All of which explains why I spent the next three hours sharing a jail cell with a hooker named Desiree.

Nearly six feet tall in her stiletto heels and Dolly Parton bouffant do, Desiree had been arrested for soliciting in the KMart parking lot. Talk about your blue light specials.

I tried not to stare at her outfit. Her bustier top was straight out of *Moulin Rouge*, and if her miniskirt had been any shorter it would've been a belt.

"What're you in for?" she asked, pushing back the cuticles on her inch-long nails.

"Attempted burglary. But it's a ghastly mistake. I didn't do anything."

"Me, neither," she said, loudly, so the cop on duty could hear. "I was just shopping for underwear."

Yeah, right. If she was wearing underwear, I was wearing the Hope diamond.

"I can't help it if some stranger started feeling me up in the parking lot. Right, honey?"

"Uh, right," I said, not wanting to offend a six foot tall hooker whose fingernails would qualify as lethal weapons in an airport security check.

As the minutes sped by like hours, Desiree and I struck up a friendship. She told me about her ex-husband, a charming fellow who liked to shoot rats at the city dump, and I told her about The Blob, and how his rear end was surgically attached to our La-Z-Boy. We both agreed we were much better off single.

It turned out that Desiree's real name was Martha Dubyk, and that her lifelong dream was to become a professional psychic.

"I've got a real gift," she said. "I can see the future clear as if it was on TV."

"Is that so?"

"I worked at the Psychic Hotline for a while, but you make more money at phone sex."

Who says jail isn't educational?

"Some day when I've saved up enough dough, I'm gonna open a little salon on Sunset Plaza, where the rich people go. I'm gonna be a Psychic to the Stars."

Then she sidled up to me, so close I could smell the Juicy Fruit on her breath.

"In fact," she whispered, "I once gave a reading to Mr. X." She named a Hollywood star famous for his action flicks. "Of course, I was on my back at the time. But he was very impressed."

"I'm sure he was."

"Say, how about I do you?"

For a frightening minute, I thought she was propositioning me. But then I realized she merely wanted to predict my future.

She took my hands in hers, the better to feel my "emanations," and, after much sighing and hand squeezing, told me that I'd soon be hearing from my long-lost sister, that my parents wanted me to know they were well and happy in heaven, and that I was about to take up a career in the medical profession.

"Wow. That's amazing," I said.

And it was. She got absolutely everything wrong. For one thing, I don't have a sister. For another, as you well know, my parents are alive and nutty in Tampa Vistas. And just the thought of going to the doctor's office for a routine checkup gives me the heebie jeebies.

I just hoped she kept her day job.

We shot the breeze a while longer. I told Desiree about my life as a writer of industrial brochures, and Desiree told me how to make a guy reach orgasm in thirty seconds or less.

Finally, a cop came over to our cell and said I was free to go. Lt. Webb had called and vouched for me. I bid Desiree a fond farewell and headed outside to breathe the fresh air of freedom.

I wasn't out in the fresh air of freedom for two seconds when I realized I had no way of getting back home. My car was still out in Ocean Park.

So I went back inside to a pay phone and called Kandi.

"You're where?" she shrieked, when I told her where I was.

"At the Van Nuys jail," I repeated.

"What're you doing in jail?"

"Getting sex tips from a hooker."

"What?"

"I'll explain everything when I see you."

I asked if she could tear herself away from the adventures of *Beanie & the Cockroach* and pick me up.

"Don't worry, sweetie. I'll be right there."

Which wasn't exactly true. It took her forty minutes to drive over from the studio, which left me plenty of time to sit on the front steps of the jail, breathing the fresh air of freedom, along with the carcinogens from the passing traffic.

"You poor thing!" Kandi said when she saw me. She put her arms around me and gave me a comforting hug.

"Phew," she said, breaking away. "You smell just like rancid seaweed. What on earth happened?"

I gave her the *Reader's Digest* version of my adventures.

I told her about how I'd been walking on the beach trying to figure out who on earth could've killed SueEllen, and how I'd stepped in a seaweedy wave, and how I was spying on Eduardo when he caught me and was about to drag me to his studio when the cops showed up and thought I was a burglar, and how they threw me in jail with Desiree, and that I was certain Eduardo was a killer who'd stop at nothing to keep the world from discovering the black lace panties in his underwear drawer.

"Holy Moses," she said, when I was through.

My sentiments exactly.

"Desiree really slept with Mr. X?"

"Focus, Kandi. That's not the main point. The main point is that Eduardo Jensen was the blonde Heidi saw on the day of the murder."

By now we were inching along on the 405 freeway. There are times when it's smooth sailing on the 405. Those times are usually between 3 and 3:05 a.m. The rest of the time, it's the world's longest parking lot. Kandi, always an impatient driver, was weaving in and out of the crawling stream, trying to catch the fastest lane.

"No," she said, "the main point is you almost got killed. I told you this investigation was dangerous."

"You were right," I acknowledged.

"Now I hope you'll listen to me when I tell you to . . . buzz off, jerkhead!"

"What?"

"Sorry, I was talking to that idiot in the

BMW. Did you see the way he cut me off? Damn BMW drivers.

"I hope you choke on your cell phone!" she shouted out the window.

And then she burst out crying.

"Kandi, honey, it's nothing to cry over. Just another self-centered BMW driver. There are millions of them out there."

"No, it's not that. It's that creep Matt."

Uh-oh. I smelled trouble on the Love Boat.

"How could I have been foolish enough to fall for a guy who waxes his chest hair?"

"He waxes his chest hair?"

"Says it cuts down on drag time when he's swimming laps. Anyhow, remember I told you he had something important he wanted to ask me? Guess what it was."

Something told me it wasn't, *Will you marry me?*

"He wanted to know if I was interested in investing in a tae kwon do studio."

"What a jerk."

"It gets worse. After dinner, we went on one of his irritating after-dinner walks. He was so damn annoying with all that constant exercising. So there we were, walking along on a quiet side street, when we heard footsteps coming up behind us. We turned around and saw a huge guy with a shaved head and tattoos up and down his arms. I swear, he looked like an escaped convict."

"Yikes."

"The guy glared at Matt and said, *I need cash.* Now normally I would have been terrified, but I wasn't really scared because Matt is a martial arts expert. I figured, *Haha, you lowlife thug. You've met your match.* But Matt took one look at the guy, and you'll never guess what he did."

Something told me the answer wasn't, *Beat him to a pulp.*

"He took one look at the guy, and started running."

"No!"

"Yes! He left me all alone with this ghastly thug."

"My God," I gasped. "What did you do?"

"What could I do? I handed him my purse and said — Move your ass, you stupid moron!"

"You said that to the thug?"

"No, no. I was talking to that idiot in the Camry.

"If you were going any slower," she shouted to the car in front of us, "you'd be going backwards!

"Anyhow," she said, resuming her story, "it turned out he wasn't a convict. He was a Romanian exchange student, and he'd ran out of gas. With his thick accent, it came out sounding like 'cash.' He just wanted to know where the nearest gas station was."

"Oh, honey. What an incredible ordeal."

Of course, there was a bright side to all this. At least I wouldn't have to sit through any more *Isn't Matt Wonderful?* stories.

"Can you believe he ran off and left me like that? And I didn't even have my car."

"How did you get home?"

"Oh, Stanislau gave me a lift."

"Stanislau?"

"The Romanian exchange student. He's actually very nice. He's taking me to the movies Sunday. And afterwards we're going to his favorite Romanian restaurant.

"You know," she said, giving the finger to a dawdler in an adjacent Cadillac, "I've always been fascinated with the Slavic nations."

I sat back and took advantage of the lull before the onslaught of *Isn't Stanislau Wonderful?* stories.

Kandi dropped me off at my Corolla, where I was thrilled to find a $60 parking ticket propped on the windshield. A little gift from the city of Los Angeles.

But the day was about to take a turn for the better. Because when I got back to my apartment, there was a message from Lt. Webb on my machine.

The cops had shown up at Eduardo's just in time to find him burning the wig in his fireplace. Fortunately, they were able to fish out a large portion of it unscathed by flames.

Not only that, but the gallery owner who'd given Eduardo his alibi confessed that he'd been lying to protect his client. When the cops put the squeeze on him, he admitted Eduardo had been nowhere near Santa Barbara on the day of the murder.

"Thanks so much, Jaine," Webb said on the machine. "We really couldn't have broken this case without you."

I played the message three times just to hear those words.

"Did you hear that, Prozac?" I said, scooping her up in my arms. "They couldn't have broken the case without me!"

Whew! Ever hear of deodorant? was what she was no doubt thinking as she wriggled free from my loving embrace.

And she was right. It was definitely time to wash up. And then I realized with a surge of joy: At last it was safe to go back to the bathroom!

Oh, happy day.

I tootled off to the bathroom, peeling off my clothes en route.

I opened the bathroom door and gasped. No, I didn't see another hair dryer in the tub. But I did see myself in the mirror. Not a pretty picture. Think Medusa on a bad hair day.

Too exhausted for a bath, I took a quick shower. Standing under the hot spray, I felt all the tension of the past few days drain out of my body. I emerged from the shower, squeaky clean, smelling of Ivory soap instead of Eau de Seaweed.

I slipped into my ancient pink chenille bathrobe and fed Prozac an early dinner of Savory Beef Guts. Then I unplugged the phone and collapsed into bed.

It had been one heck of a day. My first time in jail. My first ride in a squad car. My first encounter with a psychic hooker. And most amazing of all, I realized just before I drifted off to sleep, the first time I'd spent a day without eating. It's true. I hadn't eaten a thing since that Egg McMuffin I'd picked up for breakfast. For one whole day, I'd actually forgotten about food.

Quick, somebody call Ripley's Believe It or Not.

YOU'VE GOT MAIL!

To: Jausten
From: Shoptillyoudrop
Subject: Back from Ohio

Well, honey, we're back from Ohio, and all I can say is, I can never show my face in that state again.

The wedding was a nightmare.

Remember Charleton MacAfee, whose name was on the wedding invitation? Well, it turns out that Charleton is cousin Cindy's dog! A hunting spaniel. Cindy and her husband, who are incidentally every bit as crazy as Uncle Fred and Aunt Earlene, decided they wanted the dog to be in the wedding party.

So Charleton was the ring bearer! I'm not kidding, honey. The dog walked down the aisle with a little basket hanging from his neck, with the ring inside.

He was perfectly well behaved until he saw your father's toupee. Then all hell broke loose. He leaped up on Daddy's shoulders and grabbed the toupee in his mouth, and after chewing it to shreds, started racing up and down the aisle with the remains in his mouth. I'm sure he thought it was a squirrel.

313

Finally Cindy managed to grab him, but not before he ripped her wedding veil. Then your father threatened to sue Uncle Fred, and before you know it, they were throwing punches at each other, only unfortunately Daddy wound up hitting the minister by mistake, and somebody called the police. I'm afraid the "bottom line" as you people out in Hollywood say, is that we may be getting sued by the United Methodist Church of Ohio.

On the plus side, that hideous toupee is chewed beyond recognition. I told your father that if he bought another toupee, I was leaving him. And that seemed to put the fear of God in him. He's been quiet as a mouse, very kind and considerate; he even cleaned out the garage like I've been begging him to for months. And to make amends, he's booked us on a two-week cruise to Bermuda.

So I guess all's well that ends well. That is, if the church doesn't sue us.

Love from,
Mom

To: Jausten
From: DaddyO
Subject: A Fabulous Product

Hi, pumpkin. Mother may have mentioned the teeny little upset at Cousin Cindy's wedding. It wasn't nearly as bad as she says, but she's been under a lot of stress lately, so I've booked us on a cruise to Bermuda.

Incidentally, I've been giving a lot of thought to what you wrote the other day, and I've decided to give up wearing a toupee. It's really not worth the bother.

Instead, I've ordered a fabulous product I saw on an infomercial. It's like Christmas tree flocking. Only you spray it on your bald spot, and voila — it looks just like hair. I haven't told your mother about it. I think I'll surprise her with it on the cruise.

Chapter Twenty-Three

I woke up the next morning to the sweet sounds of Prozac howling for her breakfast. And considering that I hadn't eaten in nearly twenty-four hours, I was a tad hungry myself. In fact, I came *this close* to nibbling on Prozac's Fancy Fish Entrails. But you'll be happy to know I did the sensible thing and ate some martini olives instead.

Then I threw on my jeans and a sweatshirt and drove over to Junior's Deli, where I treated myself to bacon and eggs, french fries, and a toasted English muffin with strawberry jam.

Okay, two English muffins. With extra jam. I was famished.

I was just tucking into the first half of my second muffin when I looked up and saw an old man at the next table reading the morning paper. I could see the headline clearly: *Local Artist Arrested in Kingsley Murder.*

"Hey, I broke that case!" I wanted to shout. But instead, I just asked the waitress for some more strawberry jam.

After breakfast, topped off by a free candy-striped mint from the cashier, I got in the Corolla and headed off to buy a new hair dryer. I was getting tired of looking like I'd just stuck my finger in a light socket.

Having nabbed a good 14 hours of shuteye, you would think I'd had enough sleep to last me for a week, but strangely enough, when I got home, I was still tired. Which is why I got back in my robe, and spent the rest of the morning curled up in bed watching an old Marx Brothers movie on TV. If you ask me, Groucho Marx was a comic genius. Although Prozac insists that Harpo was the funny one.

I finally managed to pry myself out of bed and check my e-mail. I deleted the generous offers to add inches to my penis, and read about my parents' disastrous adventures at Cousin Cindy's wedding. I think the surgeon general should make Daddy wear a warning label: *Living with me can be dangerous to your mental health.* Between Daddy's toupee and all the wigs I'd been encountering lately, it seemed like my life had been taken over by hairpieces.

I was just about to climb back in bed and watch a lady on HGTV make lampshades out of leftover wallpaper, when I remembered that I'd unplugged the phone last night. No wonder it had been so quiet all morning. No sooner had I plugged it back in than it rang.

It was Lt. Webb.

"Are you okay?" he asked. "I've been calling all morning."

"I'm fine."

"I just wanted to thank you again for all your help in this case."

I was glad he was big enough to admit I'd played a part solving the crime. In fact, he went on for quite some time about how grateful he was until finally he said he had to get off the phone and tend to some important police business. Probably making sure they didn't forget the goat cheese on his goat cheese and cilantro pizza.

The minute I hung up, the phone rang again.

"Are you okay? I've been calling all morning."

This time it was Heidi.

I assured her that I was fine.

"Can you come over? Daddy has something he wants to give you."

My heart did a somersault. Was it possible that Hal was going to write me another check? After all, Hal Kingsley was a very rich man and I had just saved his daughter from a nasty criminal trial. Not to mention the hundreds of thousands of dollars I'd saved him in legal fees. Yes, I bet he *was* going to write me another check. Oh, wow. This was all too wonderful. At last I could afford that Jaguar I'd always dreamed of.

Now don't get me wrong. My only reason for getting involved in this case was to help Heidi. I'd never even thought about getting paid for it. But I certainly wasn't going to turn down a zero-laden check if it was offered to me.

I assured Heidi I'd be over ASAP, and hurried to the bedroom to choose an appropriate check-cashing outfit (jeans, silk blouse, and Ann Taylor blazer). Then I sped off to Casa Kingsley, visions of Jaguars dancing in my head.

Conchi greeted me at the door, and in a surprising burst of emotion, she put down her Windex bottle and threw her arms around me.

"Oh, Miss Jaine," she said. "Thank you so much for saving Miss Heidi."

"It was nothing," I said, breathing in her pungent perfume of sweat and Ammonia-D.

Eventually she released me and led me to the living room, where Heidi was sitting at the bay window, reading a book, just like the day I first saw her.

"Hey, kiddo."

"Jaine!"

She put down the book and hurried to my side. What a difference from the day we met. It wasn't just the weight she'd lost. She was happy now. I could see it in her eyes.

"Oh, Jaine," she said, hugging me. "If it weren't for you, I'd be in jail right now. How can I ever thank you?"

"Just seeing you happy is all the thanks I need."

And I meant it. At that moment, Hal's check was the furthest thing from my mind. I really liked this kid, and I was glad I'd been able to help her.

At which point, Grandma Kosciusko came bustling in the room.

"Jaine, darling!" she said, joining the hugfest.

After numerous *thank you*'s and *aw shucks, it was nothing*'s, we finally broke apart.

"Let's not waste any more time," Grandma K said. "Hal's waiting for you in his study. He has something he wants to give you."

Okay, this was it. I felt like a lottery

winner come to pick up my winnings. Grandma K led me to Hal's study. She said she and Heidi would wait for me in the den while I had my chat with her son.

Hal sat behind a fabulous antique desk in his wood-paneled study. The air was thick with the smell of expensive leather.

"Jaine," he said, looking up at me over his $500 reading glasses. "It's so good to see you. I want you to know how grateful we all are for the part you played in exonerating my daughter."

"Oh, it was nothing," I lied.

"And as a gesture of our appreciation, I've got a little gift for you."

"You didn't have to," I said, wondering if I should order the Jaguar in hunter green or black.

"There it is."

He pointed to a couple of shopping bags propped up against the wall.

Huh? What happened to my check, the one with all the zeroes?

"My daughter tells me how much you like shoes. Apparently you two went shoe shopping one day."

I nodded numbly.

"Anyhow, we were cleaning out SueEllen's closet, and we thought you might like hers. Heidi says you and Sue-

321

Ellen are the same size."

Oh, great. Just what I wanted. A dead woman's shoes.

"And there's one other thing I'd like to give you."

Good old Hal. It looked like he was going to come through for me, after all. Maybe I'd get a moonroof on the Jaguar. And a five-disk CD changer.

"You know that liposuction you wanted?" Hal beamed. "It's on the house."

Funny. I used to say I'd give all the money in the world for thin thighs. But now that they were a possibility, I realized I'd rather have all the money in the world.

"That's great," I said, wondering how much it would cost to buy new floor mats for the Corolla. "Just great."

I save the guy hundreds of thousands of dollars in legal fees, and he gives me used shoes and a liposuction. I guess that's how the rich stay rich.

I picked up my shoes and took them to the den where Heidi and Grandma K were waiting for me with cookies and cocoa. I kept up my grateful act, pretending to be excited about the shoes. But I didn't really mind. (Not much, anyway.) Like I said, I was just glad that everything had worked out so well for Heidi. We chatted a bit

322

about where Heidi was going to apply to college. Somewhere back east, she said, so she could be near Grandma Kosciusko. It was clear that these two really loved each other. It was about time Heidi had someone in her life who did.

I kissed them both goodbye, promising to keep in touch, then headed out to the Corolla.

"Looks like I won't be trading you in, after all," I said, tossing the shoes in the back seat.

I was just about to get in when Brad came charging up the driveway in his Ferrari. Why did he always seem to be showing up just as I was leaving? Maybe he planned it that way.

"Hi, Judy," he said, with a nasty little smile.

"Hi, Brat."

His smile went bye-bye.

"It's Brad," he said, through gritted teeth.

"No," I said. "It's brat. Spoiled brat."

Yes, I really did say that. And it felt great.

Chapter
Twenty-Four

"So what do you think?" I asked Prozac, modeling a pair of $1,300 Manolo Blahnik sandals.

Prozac looked up from where she was napping on the sofa, and shot me an irritated look.

Do you realize how much poached salmon you could buy me with thirteen hundred dollars?

I'd just spent the past hour trying on SueEllen's shoes. I tried on skinny slingbacks, strappy thongs, cork-soled wedgies straight out of a porno movie, and a pair of pointy black leather pumps that laced half-way up my calves, for the ever popular ballerina-dominatrix look.

Now I was prancing around in the $1,300 sandals. Yes, that's right. I almost fainted when I saw the price tag on the box. I've had cars that cost less than those shoes.

And at five hundred dollars a pop, the others weren't exactly bargains, either.

True, they were beautiful. But there was no way I was going to keep them. What was I going to wear them with? My Old Navy sweats? And where was I going to wear them? Dinner and dancing at the Jack in the Box?

I made up my mind to sell them on eBay. There were at least a dozen pairs of shoes, and if I could get two or three hundred dollars a pair, that would add up to a couple of thousand dollars. Yes, I'd get rid of them all. Except maybe the slingbacks. They'd look great with my sexy little black dress. Not that I actually owned a sexy little black dress. But I planned on buying one just as soon as I lost a dress size or three.

I tried on the slingbacks one more time. They really were fabulous. From the ankle down I was the spitting image of Sarah Jessica Parker.

It was at that moment that Prozac decided one of the shoe boxes was her mortal enemy. She lunged at it with the same ferocity she usually saves for my pantyhose. You've seen those nature films on the Discovery Channel where lions attack poor little gazelles? Well, Prozac went at that shoebox like a lioness on speed. I quickly grabbed it from her.

"What do you think you're doing?" I admonished her.

She shot me a dirty look, and jumped back on the sofa to resume her nap.

I was looking at the shoe box to see how badly she'd damaged it, when I noticed what looked like a photo peeking out from the tissue paper at the bottom of the box. I reached in and pulled it out. It was a faded picture of two tow-headed girls standing barefoot in front of a rundown house. The girls, in their late teens, were dressed for a special occasion, in cheap frilly dresses.

One of the girls was ordinary, short and squat, with a square face and limp hair. The other — in spite of her cheap dress and bare feet — was a knockout. Tall and willowy, with a beaming Prom Queen smile, she looked boldly into the camera. I'd know that face anywhere. It was Sue-Ellen, the high school version. I flipped the picture over. On the back it said *SueEllen and Carolee. Graduation Day.*

I wondered who Carolee was. Probably a friend. Or a relative. Whoever she was, she was totally eclipsed by SueEllen's radiance.

I took a closer look at the house behind them. It was straight out of *Tobacco Road*, with a sagging front porch and termite-eaten shutters. I remembered what Sue-Ellen had said about growing up in genteel poverty. What a crock. From the looks of that house and the dress she was wearing, SueEllen was no Southern belle. She was plain old trailer trash.

How ironic, I thought, that Hal and Sue-Ellen wound up together. Hal with his phony Anglo name, and SueEllen with her fictional landed gentry ancestors. I could just picture them in the early days of their courtship, pretending to be something they weren't. Each of them falling in love with someone who didn't exist.

I pulled out the rest of the tissue paper in the shoebox, wondering if anything else had been buried there. Indeed there was — a letter, addressed to SueEllen in a shaky hand. But this was no memento from the past. It was postmarked from Georgia, just a few months ago. I debated the ethics of reading it for a whole nanosecond, then dived right in.

SueEllen, honey — Hope you are well and happy. Wish I could say the same for myself. The cancer is spreading, and the pain is something awful. I'll be glad when it's over. And that's why I'm writing to you. You've always been my favorite niece, so much more fun than your sister Carolee. And so I'm leaving all my money to you. Close to three million dollars, after taxes. I just wanted you to know, in case Carolee tries to pull any funny business. I wouldn't put it past her. Lots of love, pussycat, from your Aunt Melanie.

So SueEllen really did have a rich Aunt Melanie. That part of her past was true. But she'd lied about being an only child. She had a sister named Carolee. No wonder she kept it a secret. A sister with a hillbilly accent and dirt between her toes would be an ugly blot on the genteel portrait of her past that SueEllen had so carefully painted.

Had Hal ever found out the truth about SueEllen, I wondered, or did he still think she'd grown up sipping juleps among the magnolia blossoms? Should I let him know about the picture, and spoil his illusions? Yet somehow I didn't think Hal had many illusions about SueEllen. I was pretty sure he'd stopped loving her a long time ago. He'd probably toss the picture in the trash without a second thought.

But then again, maybe he wouldn't.

Maybe he cared for her more than I thought. Maybe he'd want to have this keepsake from her past. And surely I had to tell him about the letter. What if he was next in line to cash in on that three million dollars?

I tried calling him, but he wasn't in. Conchi told me that he'd taken the kids for dinner at the In 'N Out Burger.

"The In 'N Out Burger? SueEllen's probably rolling over in her grave."

"Si, I know," Conchi chuckled.

I told her to tell Hal I'd found the picture of SueEllen and her sister, and to please call me when he got in.

Then I hung up and looked around the living room. Shoe boxes were scattered everywhere, like Christmas morning at Imelda Marcos's house. Oh, well. I'd clean up later. Right now, all I wanted was a nice relaxing soak in the tub. It felt like ages since I'd had one.

I started the water running, and tossed in a handful of strawberry-scented bath salts. Then I turned on the radio to a soothing classical music station, and headed for the kitchen to pour myself a tall cool glass of chardonnay.

I was on my way back to the bathroom when I saw the picture of SueEllen on the coffee table. I decided to bring it in the tub with me. Something about SueEllen in her redneck years fascinated me. By the time I got back to the bathroom, the tub was filled with a lovely mountain of strawberry-scented bubbles. I slipped out of my clothes, and eased myself into the steamy water. Then I took a sip of my wine and sighed with pleasure.

"Who needs a man," I asked Prozac, who was perched on top of the toilet tank, "when you've got a hot bath and a cold chardonnay?"

Certainly not me, she seemed to be saying, licking her privates with gusto.

Then I reached for the picture of SueEllen. God, she was a knockout. Even in that crappy dress and bad haircut. She was one of those irritating women who go straight from adorable child to spectacular adult, totally bypassing any awkward stages. Unlike her sister. Poor Carolee. With her squat body, and plain features, she certainly was the loser in that gene pool.

Yet there was something about her face that looked familiar. Where had I seen it before? While SueEllen smiled boldly at the camera, Carolee looked at the ground with downcast eyes. They were like two characters from a fairy tale. SueEllen, the princess. Carolee, the lowly servant girl. And that's when it hit me. I knew who that face belonged to. The servant who was always looking down at the ground, afraid to make eye contact. It was *Conchi,* with blond hair. Yes, the resemblance was undeniable.

Conchi was SueEllen's sister Carolee. The same Carolee who'd just been aced out of Aunt Melanie's will. What had Aunt Melanie written in her letter? That she was afraid Carolee might try to pull some "funny business." What if Aunt Melanie was right, and the funny business was murder?

What if Aunt Melanie had left all her money to SueEllen, but SueEllen wasn't around to collect it? If Carolee was next in line as beneficiary, she would have had the perfect motive for murder.

I sat up abruptly in the tub, and took another slug of my chardonnay. Maybe the cops had arrested the wrong person. Maybe Eduardo was innocent. Maybe he hadn't been trying to kill me. Maybe he was just some crazy transvestite who'd tried to scare me into keeping his secret.

Suddenly the chardonnay turned to bile in my throat. I remembered the phone call

I'd made just a little while ago. I'd told Conchi about the picture. Surely she'd figure out that I might recognize her. If she really did kill SueEllen, then she wouldn't hesitate to kill me. I had to call Lt. Webb right away. And then I had to grab Prozac and get the hell out of my apartment.

But it was too late.

Because just then I looked up and saw Conchi standing in the doorway, a gun in her hand. No longer a dark-haired Latina, but a blonde.

"You really should keep your windows locked," she said, aiming the gun straight at my heart.

Chapter
Twenty-Five

Don't you just hate it when you're having a nice relaxing soak in the tub, and a murderer shows up?

I don't know about you, but I for one was in an advanced state of panic. All I could think of was that I'd be naked when the cops discovered my body. If only I'd gone to Weight Watchers! If only I'd joined a gym! If only I hadn't turned on that damn radio! Then I would've heard Conchi coming and escaped through the bathroom window. These were the thoughts that raced through my mind as I stared into the barrel of Conchi's gun.

"Well, if it isn't Miss Jaine," she said. Her Spanish accent was gone, replaced by a Southern drawl.

"Hey, Conchi," I said, trying not to sound as terrified as I felt. "I almost didn't recognize you without your Windex."

Conchi laughed. "That was a nice touch, wasn't it? Made me look ever so much more servile. And by the way, it's Carolee, not Conchi."

"I know."

"Too bad you found the picture. I was hoping I wouldn't have to kill you."

"I think you should know," I said, trying to keep my voice from quivering, "that my neighbor can hear everything that goes on in my apartment.

"Lance!" I shouted. "Call the cops! Right now!"

"Nice try, honey. I saw him leave five minutes ago. With a handsome redheaded guy."

Damn that Jim.

I slumped back down into the tub.

"So you figured out I'm SueEllen's sister?"

I nodded numbly.

"And I saw Aunt Melanie's letter on your coffee table, so you probably know about her will, too."

I nodded again.

"Miserable bitch," she said. "Always treated me like dirt, because I wasn't pretty like SueEllen. I'm glad she's suffering now. If anyone deserves stomach cancer, she does."

"Is she still alive?"

"Just barely. Any day now, she's going to

kick the bucket. And now that SueEllen isn't around, I inherit everything. Three million dollars." She grinned like a kid in a three-million dollar candy store. "The old bat had to turn a hell of a lot of tricks for three million dollars."

I blinked in surprise. Aunt Melanie, turning tricks? What was she talking about?

"I thought Melanie was a society lady."

Conchi had a hearty chuckle over that one.

"Are you kidding? She ran the biggest whorehouse south of the Mason-Dixon line."

So SueEllen had lied about that, too.

"Aunt Melanie had the nerve to actually show me the will. She laughed when she told me she'd be leaving everything to SueEllen. *Cheer up,* she said. *Who knows? Maybe SueEllen will die before I do. And then you'll get everything.*

"Right then and there, I knew I had to get rid of SueEllen. So I bought myself a black wig, went to Berlitz and learned Spanish, and got myself a job working for Mr. and Mrs. Hal Kingsley.

"Me llamo Conchi," she said, in a mocking singsong Spanish.

"And that's not the only change I made.

I don't know if you noticed," she said, preening, "but I've lost a lot of weight since that picture."

In fact, I had noticed.

"Slimfast," she said. "You should try it. On second thought," she added, waving the gun, "I guess you won't have time for that. Anyhow, SueEllen was so damn self involved, she never even realized I was her own sister."

I could see how that could happen, how a new head of hair could totally change a person's appearance. I remembered what my mother said about Daddy, how he looked like a different person with his toupee.

"I wondered why you were always looking down at the ground," I said. "I thought it was because you were frightened. But that wasn't it. You just didn't want anyone to recognize you."

"That's right, honey. I kept a low profile. And then, when the moment was right, I took off my black wig and headed down the hallway to SueEllen's bathroom. She recognized me then, all right. Almost didn't have to toss that dryer into the tub. She practically had a heart attack right on the spot. She tried to get out of the tub, of course, but I'm a lot stronger than she was.

It was easy to push her back in. She begged me not to kill her, told me she'd split Aunt Melanie's money with me, but I believed that like I believe in the tooth fairy. I threw in the dryer and watched her fry."

I flinched at her choice of words.

"So you were the blonde Heidi saw in the hallway."

"None other."

"And you planted a blond wig in her closet to incriminate her."

"I bought it at one of those kiosks in the mall. Hated to do it to the kid, but I needed somebody to be arrested for the murder. I figured Hal would manage to get her off somehow."

Ironic, isn't it? All along, I'd been focusing on that blond wig, when it was a black one I should have been looking for.

"Now all I have to do is give my notice to the Kingsleys and head back home to collect my three million."

"You splitting it with your boyfriend, the gardener? The one who gave you your alibi?"

"No way, Jose. Any day now, he's going to meet with a fatal accident. Just like you."

"What are you going to do? Drop another hair dryer in my tub?"

"Nah. The radio will do."

Damn that infernal radio.

She started towards it, her gun aimed at my chest.

Just then I caught a glimpse of Prozac, still perched on the toilet bowl. Sensing impending danger, her eyes were wide, her ears erect. Realizing no doubt that this strange woman in our bathroom was about to do me harm, the brave little soul put her tail between her legs and whizzed out of there like greased lightning.

Conchi whirled around in surprise. She had no idea the cat had even been there. I took advantage of the moment to pull the rug out from under her. Literally. I grabbed the bathmat Conchi was standing on, and yanked it with all my might, sending her sprawling to the ground.

As she fell, she hit her head on the toilet bowl. It looked like she was unconscious, but I wasn't going to stick around to make sure. Instead I grabbed her gun and dashed out into the living room to call the cops. But before I could finish dialing 911, Conchi came lunging out of the bathroom, not the least bit unconscious, after all. With a running leap, she tackled me from behind, sending the gun flying across the room.

Oh, God. What was I going to do now? I tried to remember what Kandi had said about subduing an attacker. Gouge out their groin, and kick them in the eye? No, no. It was gouge out their eye, and kick them in the groin.

I tried the groin thing, but it didn't seem to make an impression. Before I knew it she was on top of me, her hands around my neck, trying to strangle me. And all I could think of was that scene in *Dial M for Murder* when the killer is trying to strangle Grace Kelly, and she grabs a pair of sewing scissors and stabs him in the back. Why, oh, why hadn't I ever taken up sewing?

Frantically, I groped around for something, anything, to use as a weapon. At last my fingers found one of SueEllen's shoes — a cork-soled wedgie. I grabbed it and, with all the strength I could muster, I whacked Conchi over the head.

You'll be happy to know it was a very effective blunt instrument. Conchi instantly went limp. But just to be safe, I conked her again. This time I was pretty sure she was unconscious. But I'd seen too many movies where, just when you think the bad guy is dead, he springs back to life with renewed vigor and attacks the good guy. Which is why I promptly proceeded to bind her hands and legs with several pairs of my control top pantyhose.

Still not taking any chances, I sat on her chest while I called the police. I told them someone had just tried to kill me, and they said they'd be right over.

So there I was — sitting on Conchi's chest, waiting for the cops to show up, still clutching the wedgie in case she regained consciousness — when I heard someone call my name.

"Jaine?"

I looked up, and saw Morris Pechter staring in through the open window. Oh, no! Tonight was the night we were supposed to have dinner. I'd forgotten all about it.

And now he was staring at me, wide-eyed, as I sat naked astride a bound-up Conchi, surrounded by a sea of slutty high heeled shoes.

What would my students at the Shalom Retirement Home say when they heard about this? Their esteemed teacher, a dominatrix with a shoe fetish!

Morris just stood there, gulping. After a moment, he regained his powers of speech.

"I don't know what sick game you're playing," he said.

And then he grinned sheepishly.
"But whatever it is, can I play, too?"
Damn. Another Mr. Right bites the dust.

Epilogue

Needless to say, Conchi was carted off to jail and Eduardo was released. As it turned out, getting arrested was the best thing that could have happened to Eduardo. Thanks to all the sympathetic coverage he got in the media, his paintings are more popular than ever. In fact, his latest monstrosity ("Mother Teresa in a Wonderbra") just sold for $200,000.

Hal never did marry Ginny. Or Larkspur. Or Denise. Instead, he tied the knot with a twenty-two-year-old aerobics instructor at his gym. Heidi tells me she's a bit of a birdbrain, but much nicer than SueEllen. She loves to hang out at the mall with Heidi, and has bought her some really nice outfits.

Heidi's applied to Columbia University in New York, so she can be near Grandma Kosciusko. Meanwhile, she and I get together for lunch on Saturdays. Afterwards we go to the Museum of TV and Radio. Heidi's given up watching *Bachelor Father*.

Perhaps in anticipation of her future adventures as a single gal in New York, her sitcom of choice nowadays is *That Girl*.

After getting drunk one night at a Sunset Strip club, Brad Kingsley totalled his Ferrari. I'm happy to report that he walked away with only a few scratches. I'm even happier to report that Hal refused to buy him another Ferrari. Nowadays Brad is tooling around town in a Corolla, just like mine. Talk about your poetic justice.

Oh, yes. And three days after the accident, Amber left him for a USC senior with a Maserati.

As for Hal's ex-lovers, Larkspur O'Leary is still pounding the cellulite out of rich ladies' thighs. Ginny is dating a guy she met in the men's department at Bloomie's. And the last I heard, Denise quit her job in Hal's office and is now working for a cosmetic dentist in Van Nuys, not too far from the Van Nuys jail.

And speaking of the Van Nuys jail, I've got great news about Desiree the Hooker. Her dream of becoming a professional psychic came true. Not long ago she sent me a discount coupon for a palm reading at her new salon. And I'm actually thinking of going. Remember how she told me I'd soon be hearing from a long-lost sister?

Well, she was right. I did hear from a long-lost sister. Not mine, of course, but SueEllen's. So maybe she's good at this psychic stuff, after all.

Kandi's relationship with Stanislau didn't last very long; apparently Romanian food gave her indigestion. And poor Lance. After six months of frantic dating, his boyfriend Jim went back to his wife.

In the Some Things Never Change Department, Mom is still stockpiling fake diamonds in the unlikely event of a world cubic zirconia shortage. Daddy is still screwing up the punch lines to his jokes. And Mr. Goldman still insists that Queen Elizabeth had a nose job.

Morris never told Mrs. Pechter about finding me naked on top of Conchi. He didn't have to. One of the cops leaked the story to the L.A. *Times.* So all of greater Los Angeles read about that little escapade. I was just glad there were no accompanying pictures.

Everyone considers me a hero, though. Except for Prozac, of course, who still considers me her maid. Which reminds me, I've got to go and open a can of fancy fish guts. Talk to you later.